Praise for the uplifting novels of
ReShonda Tate Billingsley

I KNOW I'VE BEEN CHANGED

#1 *Dallas Morning News* bestseller

"Grabs you from the first page and never lets go. . . . One of the best reads of the year. Bravo!"

—Victoria Christopher Murray

"An excellent novel with a moral lesson to boot. . . . Billingsley grows as a writer with each effort."

—Zane, *New York Times* bestselling author

"This emotionally charged novel will not easily be forgotten."

—*Romantic Times* (4½ stars, Gold Medal, Top Pick)

"A compelling, heartfelt story."

—*Booklist*

LET THE CHURCH SAY AMEN

#1 *Essence* bestseller and *Dallas Morning News* bestseller

One of *Library Journal*'s Best Christian Books for 2004

"Billingsley infuses her text with just the right dose of humor to balance the novel's serious events. . . . Will appeal to fans of Michele Andrea Bowen's *Second Sunday* and Pat G'Orge-Walker's *Sister Betty! God's Calling You Again!*"

—*Library Journal* (starred review)

"Her community of very human saints will win readers over with their humor and verve."

—*Booklist*

"Amen to *Let the Church Say Amen*. . . . [A] well-written novel."

—*Indianapolis Recorder*

Also by ReShonda Tate Billingsley

My Brother's Keeper
Let the Church Say Amen
I Know I've Been Changed
Four Degrees of Heat
(with Brenda L. Thomas, Crystal Lacey Winslow and
Rochelle Alers)
Have a Little Faith
(with Jacquelin Thomas, J. D. Mason and Sandra Kitt)

everybody
say
amen

ReShonda Tate Billingsley

POCKET BOOKS

New York   London   Toronto   Sydney

POCKET BOOKS
a Division of Simon & Schuster, Inc.
1230 Avenue of the Americas, New York, NY 10020

POCKET and colophon are registered trademarks of Simon & Schuster, Inc.

ISBN: 978-0-7394-8661-0

Manufactured in the United States of America

For my grandmothers . . . the roots that have allowed me to grow

Acknowledgments

I am so blessed. And of course I have to first give praises to God, who just keeps on blessing me and helps me achieve and realize things others only dream about.

I look at how far I've come in this literary journey and I know that I wouldn't have done it without the love, support, and encouragement of my husband, Dr. Miron Billingsley. Thank you for helping me realize my dream; know that I'm right there as you work to realize yours.

To my babies . . . Mya Simone and Morgan Camille. I began this journey when you were in the womb. Now, you are the fuel that keeps me moving along this road. Know that everything I do—I do for you. If you could just learn to be okay with people "taking Mommy's books." Mya, my proudest moment was when you wrote your first book so you could be "just like Mommy."

To my mother, Nancy . . . I've come a long way from the four-page letters that I used to write to you in high school to express myself. Thank you for struggling to give us a better life. You laid the foundation. I can't wait until I can repay you (I can hear you now—"I can't wait for you to repay me, either.").

Tanisha . . . more than ever, you and Mom helped me get this book done by taking the girls so I could make it do what it do. Thank you for being a Jill-of-all-trades. Keep pushing my books and you just might get that new car yet. (Why is it when relatives think you're doing all right, they want you to buy them something major—a house, a car? Whatever happened to "Can you buy me a new pair of shoes?" . . . But I digress.)

To two of my very best friends, Jaimi Canady and Raquelle Lewis . . . thank you for always being there for me, supporting all of my dreams, and not mistaking my lack of time for a lack of love. Jaimi, you told me you always felt God had a higher calling for me. I've found it.

To Pat "Speed Writer" Tucker Wilson. I could spend the next ten pages thanking you for all you've done for me . . . the hours and hours of conversations; you keeping me grounded and sane with everything from the TV station to the literary industry. There are very few people in this world I know I can call at the drop of a dime about anything and they're there. You're one of them. I told you your time was coming. Now do your thang.

To my wonderful, spectacular, fabulous, phenomenal, dynamic (former) editor, Selena James (can you tell I have mad love for her?). Thank you so much for nurturing me on this literary journey and listening with a straight face as I brainstormed endless ideas that sometimes I know had you wanting to say, "Get real." To Brigitte Smith and Maggie Crawford, thank you so much for picking up where Selena left off and

Acknowledgments

working tirelessly to ensure that this would be the best book it could be. Special thanks also to Louise Burke, Melissa Gramstead, and the sales team. And to everyone else at Simon & Schuster/Pocket Books, thank you for believing in my work. The sky's the limit.

You know I have to give a huge, huge thanks to my agent, Sara Camilli, who is always looking out for me and believed in me way back when.

To my boys at the J-O-B, Fox 26 News: Ray Williams, Charles Hobson, Ray Ramirez, Torrey Walker, Joe McGinty, Isiah Carey (check out his blog at carey2.blogspot.com), Rodney Pearson, and Xavier Kirts. (Xavier, keep the faith—your lotto numbers will come in.) To my spiritual/business advisor, "Deacon" Todd Smith. Man, I can't thank you enough for helping me keep my head up when I felt beat down. You were there as I wrote this book, helping me to stay focused on the bigger picture and to remember above all else, rely on God when life gets you down. You are more than just a colleague. You're a friend. See you at Starbucks to broker those big deals.

To the real First Ladies who let me pick their brains and who talked to me about how a "real woman of God" should act: Luela Walker (my First Lady), Vonda Edwards, Mia Wright, Doris Childress, Doris Ratcliffe, and Kayla Simmons.

To the ministers who provide inspiration (the good stuff) for my stories: Rev. Harvey Walker (my pastor), Rev. Mark Edwards, Rev. Moses Woodruff, Jr., Rev. Terrence Johnson, Rev. KirbyJon Caldwell, Rev. Robert Childress, Bishop T. D. Jakes, Bishop Eddie Long, Rev. Remus Wright.

Acknowledgments

Thanks also to the authors who never hesitate to help a sister out: King "The world ain't ready for me" Jihad (keep your head up), Victoria Christopher Murray, Nina Foxx, Norma Jarrett, Jacqueline Thomas, Sheila Dansby Harvey, James Guittard, Carl Weber, Eric Pete, and Zane and the Strebor Family. Much love also to the other ladies of Femme Fantastik (Lori, Carmen, Trisha, and Wendy).

Now, let me get to the part that I know is going to get me in trouble because I know I'll leave someone out. But here goes . . .

Thanks so much, as always, to my sorors of Alpha Kappa Alpha Sorority, Inc., especially the Houston area chapters, including my own—Mu Kappa Omega—and my sister's chapter, Chi Omicron Omega; and to my girls who were there for me when I was making $5 an hour as an anchor in Port Arthur—Kim Wright, Clemelia Richardson, Finisha Waits, Beverly Davis, Leslie Mouton, and Trina McReynolds.

Also thanks to Deidre Lodrig, Angie Pickett Henderson, Carlos Canady, Saki Indakwa, my former co-workers at Fox 26 News, and all my other friends and family. To JeCaryous Johnson, Gary Guidry, and LaKeysha Jones at I'm Ready Productions and Keith Davis and Deshawn Colbert at DMARS.

Thanks to the schools and churches that have already had me out and allowed me to do what I do best—inspire and motivate young people; especially Contemporary Learning Center; Madison, Kashmere, and Westside High Schools; Christa McAuliffe Middle School; Klentzman Intermediate; Alief Hastings, St. Luke's, Brentwood, Brookhollow, Friendship

Acknowledgments

West, New Birth, Mt. Ararat, Mt. Horeb, and Higher Dimensions Baptist Churches; as well as Windsor Village United Methodist Church and Ft. Bend Church.

Thanks also to all the book clubs and bookstores that have shown me mad, mad love. Nnette's Book Break; Go On Girl (Texas 1) (special thanks to Betty for the Mimosa); Shades of You; Turning Pages (people are still raving about my purse); Zora Neale Hurston; Kindred Spirits; Cover 2 Cover; Cush City; Tea Rose (a bookclub with a butler—but then what else would I expect from women of your caliber?); Coffee, Tea and Read; Bsure; Ladies of Expression; Nubian Page Turners (you ladies definitely tell it like it is!); Pages Between Sistahs; Sistahs in Spirit; Black Orchids; Gwen Furr and Wal-Mart store #872; My Sisters & Me; Sistahs Who Are Reading; Mahogany Souls; and Kismet Book Clubs.

I know my acknowledgments run a bit long, but when you've been blessed to have so many wonderful people in your life . . . well, I just can't make excuses for letting them know they're appreciated. (And if I forgot your name, you're still appreciated and you love me so much you won't hold it against me, right ☺.)

Until next time, drop me a line and let me know what you think of the books.

Thanks for the love.

Peace.

ReShonda

Prologue

If looks could kill, Lester Adams would definitely be pushing up daisies.

Rachel glared at her husband and silently played her mantra in her head: *Do not act a fool. You are a strong, mature woman who has left those childish ways behind you. Whatever you do, do not act a fool.*

That had been Rachel's theme for the last five years, and had helped her out of numerous situations. It wasn't working today.

This fool must be on crack. Rachel inhaled deeply. "What did you just say?"

Lester got up and began his usual pacing as he tried to explain to his wife the reasoning behind his decision.

"It's not like this is something I just want to do on a whim," he said.

Rachel massaged her temples. She had done so well at walking the straight and narrow since she'd tied the knot. Marrying Lester had been the best decision she had ever made. He kept her grounded. No, he wasn't the most handsome thing, but he loved her unconditionally, and that love had made her want to be a better woman. But what he was saying now was absolutely insane.

"I talked this over with your father and he's pleased with the decision," Lester added nervously.

Rachel remained at a loss for words. She stared at her husband. The red pimples were gone from his sandpaper-colored skin thanks to Proactiv, and she'd convinced him to shave off the red mop that had sat on his head for years. Now he wore a closely cropped fade. Right about now, though, she wished she could grab that head of hair and shake some sense into him.

"Baby, I know you don't understand this." Lester sat down next to her. She immediately stood up. It was her turn to pace their spacious three-bedroom apartment.

"You're right. I don't," she said. "I don't believe you're standing here telling me this."

"Come on. You act like I'm telling you I had an affair or something," Lester tried to joke.

"I think I might be able to handle that better than this." Rachel shot him a look to let him know she wasn't joking.

Lester sighed. "Rachel, when the Lord calls, He calls. This is my destiny. You know how I've been telling you I was tired of insurance and felt I had a greater calling. Well, this is it."

Rachel spun on her husband. "A preacher, Lester? You want to be a preacher? Even worse, you want me to be a preacher's wife?" She stared at him as if that was the absolute craziest thing she'd ever heard.

"That's exactly what I want, Rachel."

Rachel cocked her head in confusion. "What makes you think those people at Zion Hill—'one of the most prominent churches in Houston,' as they like to boast—will let you be their preacher anyway?"

"Come on. After Reverend Wright got arrested in the pulpit, I think the board wants someone safe like me."

She could understand that much. That whole situation had been a fiasco. Deacon Wright had finally gotten his wish a year ago when Rachel's father, Rev. Simon Jackson, had stepped down as pastor of Zion Hill. The deacon was able to get his nephew, Milton Wright, in as the church's new preacher. The only problem was that Reverend Wright never informed anyone of his outstanding warrants for hot checks—more than fifty thousand dollars' worth.

The police had come and arrested him right in the middle of Sunday morning service. Wright had taken off running right in the middle of the sermon with the police chasing him all the way down the street. It was a nightmare that took Zion Hill months to live down.

But what Rachel couldn't understand was why her husband had to be the replacement. "Since when did you even want to be a preacher? Besides, you haven't been to theology school or anything."

Lester sighed in frustration. "Not every minister is trained in the Word. For some, it's just a calling."

"You really think those people at Zion Hill will let somebody with no experience be their preacher?"

"I've been a member of that church since I was born, Rachel. They support what I'm doing wholeheartedly. They know me and they don't have to worry about any mess like what happened with Reverend Wright. And it's not like I'll just jump in the pulpit. Your father has agreed to mentor me. I can also take part in a six-week theological seminar. And I'll work closely with the deacon board."

"Lester, this is insane." Rachel tried to reason with him. "You can't possibly want this. Is this some early midlife crisis or something? If so, go buy a motorcycle or get a tattoo."

"Rachel, if you half paid attention to me you'd know that I have always felt something was missing in my life! I've been praying on it and meeting regularly with your father about it," Lester said. "I've even preached a couple of times at different churches in the city already."

"What? When did this happen and why didn't I know anything about it?" Sure, she was wrapped up in her own little world most of the time, but surely she would've known about her husband having a desire to preach, let alone actually having preached somewhere.

Lester cast his eyes downward. "You never show an interest in what I'm doing. I didn't want to hear you try to talk me out of it, so I didn't tell you what I was doing."

Rachel shook her head as she continued walking back and

forth across the room. She looked at the family photo of her, Lester, Jordan, and Nia. Both of her kids loved Lester to death. For Nia, he was the only father she'd ever known, since her real daddy didn't half fool with her. Jordan's father, Bobby, was in his life, but the nine-year-old still loved him some Daddy Lester. Rachel couldn't believe she was about to lose the happy home she'd worked so hard to build. But that was what was about to happen because there was no way on earth she would ever be a preacher's wife. She wasn't as buck wild as she used to be, but she definitely wasn't first lady material and didn't care to be first lady material. "This is too much," she said. "This is just coming out of the blue. Are you sucking up to my father, trying to be like the great Simon Jackson?"

Lester jumped to his feet, his frustrations becoming evident. "It's not like that at all. This is not a decision I've made lightly."

Rachel put a finger in the air and began wiggling her neck. She had been doing so well in keeping her ghetto ways at bay. But so much for that. "Decision? So you've already decided?"

He lowered his voice, obviously trying to remain rational. "Rachel, please understand . . ." He reached out to try and take her arm. She snatched it away.

"I'm not understanding anything!" She leaned in and pointed her index finger in his face. "You understand this. I ain't trying to be a preacher's wife. I spent my life as a preacher's daughter. I hated it growing up. The church always coming first in my family. My daddy never being around. Those holier-than-thou people watching my every move and passing judgment on me. It was horrible! But I didn't have any choice then. I have a choice about this!" She was fuming and was not about to back down. She had to let him know she meant business. Lester was a softie when it came to her. Always had been. She had to make him see this idea wasn't remotely feasible.

"What are you saying, Rachel?" Lester looked like he wanted to cry.

"What does it sound like?" Rachel stared defiantly at her husband.

"It sounds like you're giving me an ultimatum: either you or the Lord."

Rachel didn't budge. "You can make it sound as horrible as you want, I'm just telling you, I ain't trying to be a preacher's wife. Let me rephrase that. I'm *not* gon' be a preacher's wife."

Lester inhaled deeply before speaking. He looked her in the eye. "And I am telling *you*," he said, his voice taking on a strength she'd never heard, "I give you everything you want and then some. I cater to your every need, your every wish. But this is something I'm not wavering on. This is my calling and if you don't like it, you can leave." With that Lester turned and stomped out of the house.

Rachel was shocked. In their five years of marriage Lester had never so much as raised his voice at her, let alone issued her an ultimatum. But he had to be confused if he thought his little temper tantrum would change her mind. He was just going to have to find another "calling," because there was no way in hell she was going to be a preacher's wife.

chapter 1

Rachel adjusted the brim of her huge lavender hat. She brushed down her lavender suit as she surveyed her reflection in the floor-length mirror. Her auburn-tinted hair rested comfortably on her shoulders. She had to admit she was looking good.

"Girl, you make a bomb first lady," she muttered to her reflection. She couldn't help but smile. If her mother wasn't already dead, this was a sight that would have surely killed her. Nope, never in a million years would Loretta Jackson have believed her only daughter was decked out in her Sunday best, preparing to take her spot next to her husband at Zion Hill's Pastor Appreciation ceremony.

Rachel was having a hard time believing it herself. She'd

actually left Lester a year and a half ago when he didn't give in to her ultimatum. But after one week of living with her father, she returned home. Besides the fact that Simon still didn't have cable, he spent every day telling her how wrong she'd been to walk out on her husband, trying to preach to her about how Lester was doing the right thing and how she was being unreasonable. Then, to top things off, her brother, David, was living at home and his crackhead girlfriend, Tawny, was always coming around begging for another chance.

David had gotten hooked on drugs after an injury ended his promising football career. But after his mother died seven years ago, he quit cold turkey. He said he'd been clean since then; everyone else believed him, but Rachel wasn't quite sure that she did.

Plus, even though her other brother, Jonathan, had his own apartment, he was forever at Simon's, too. That place was like Grand Central Station.

And despite what she told herself, she had missed Lester something terrible.

"Hey, honey. Are you ready?"

Rachel turned toward Lester. He actually looked quite dapper in his three-piece navy suit. Nia was clutching his hand tightly. They stood in the doorway of the master bedroom, looking like the perfect father and daughter.

"Wow, Mommy, you look so pretty," Nia said. "Don't she, Daddy?"

"*Doesn't* she, sweetheart," Lester replied. "And yes, she is an absolute vision of loveliness."

"Tell me something I don't know." Rachel giggled and wiggled her hips. Nia and Lester chuckled.

"Well, we'd better get going," Lester said.

Rachel knew he was excited. Today marked his year anniversary in the pulpit and even Rachel had to admit that he was an awesome preacher. After Lester trained around the clock for six months with her father, the board agreed to offer him the job permanently. There were a couple of dissenters, but everyone knew it was personal against her father because he hadn't stepped down right after her mother died and their family drama escalated out of control. Ultimately, no one could deny what a dynamic preacher Lester was. It also didn't hurt that his grandmother was a longtime member of Zion Hill and a huge benefactor to the church.

"Where's Jordan?" Rachel asked, snapping out of her thoughts.

"Where else? In front of the TV playing that PlayStation," Lester responded.

Rachel shook her head in disgust. She'd told Jordan's father, Bobby, not to buy that dang thing. Now all Jordan ever wanted to do was play that stupid game.

Rachel followed her family downstairs and, after dragging Jordan away from the PlayStation, they headed out to church.

Fifteen minutes later, Lester navigated the family's Ford Explorer into the reserved parking spot in front of the church's back office door. Rachel noticed Sister Ida Hicks and Layla Wilson lollygagging around outside. Layla was Bobby's sister-in-law and had never liked Rachel. So Rachel made sure she took her time getting out of the car. She wanted to make an entrance.

As usual, Lester was oblivious to her showboating. He quickly made his way inside to prepare for services. Nia followed him into the building.

"Sister Wilson, you look wonderful. When is your baby due?" Rachel asked, eyeing her stomach.

Layla glared at her. "I'm not pregnant."

Rachel moved her hand to her heart. "I am so sorry. I thought I heard you were expecting."

"No. I'm not," Layla snarled.

"My apologies again." Rachel tried her best to look apologetic. She knew she was wrong. But she had overheard Layla talking about her last week and since she knew Layla was self-conscious about her plus-size frame, she couldn't help but take a dig at her.

"Hey, nephew." Layla tried to flick Rachel off as she leaned in and hugged Jordan, who was standing next to his mother. "I had a blast with you last week. Your mom can't stop talking about what a great time you, her, and your dad had."

Now it was Rachel's turn to snarl. Layla knew Rachel didn't want Jordan calling Bobby's wife, Shante, "Mom."

"Come on, Jordan," Rachel said, grabbing his hand. She ignored the snide look on Layla's face as they made their way into the church.

The choir was just beginning to sing, signaling the start of service. Rachel took her standard seat at the end of the fourth row. Much of the service was business as usual, and she had to struggle to stay focused. She nodded as her husband prepared for his sermon. He was going into that zone, the one where he concentrated on nothing but delivering an inspirational message.

She still couldn't believe she was somebody's first lady. She'd even quit her job in an upscale Galleria-area boutique to work full-time at the church handling all of the youth activities. She'd toned down some of her wild ways and was trying her best to be nicer to people. (Layla didn't count.) It had been hard adjusting at first, because she definitely wasn't used to being in church *every* Sunday, and especially not on time. But she'd adjusted a lot better than she'd thought she would. Still, Rachel already knew some things were gon' have to change around Zion Hill. She'd been patient, trying to let Lester get acclimated, but it was time for her to do *her* thing.

"Good morning, church!" Lester said as he stepped up to the podium. "Have I got a message for you today!"

Rachel couldn't help but smile. Lester definitely seemed to have found his calling in the pulpit. It was like he came alive. No, it was like he became a totally different person. She, on the other hand, always found her mind wandering to a million other things, but she'd learned to plaster on a smile and throw in a couple of nods and "Amens" for good measure, so no one ever really knew.

Lester must've been fifteen minutes into his sermon when a loud shout broke Rachel out of her mental trance.

"Take it back you pig-faced punk!"

Lester abruptly stopped preaching and—along with everyone else—directed his attention to the pew where the ruckus was coming from.

"I ain't taking nothing back. My mama said yo' mama is a tramp and your uncle is a fag."

Before anyone could move, Jordan jumped from his seat, pounced on Sister Hicks's ten-year-old great-grandson, who was sitting next to him, and pummeled the boy's face.

"Lawd, have mercy," someone muttered.

"Jesus, they fighting in the Lord's house," someone else said.

Both Rachel and Lester raced toward Jordan at the same time. It took both of them and three deacons to pull the boys apart.

"Let me go! Let me go! I'ma kick his funky butt!" Jordan shouted.

Rachel heard several members gasp. But she couldn't deal with them right now. "Jordan!" she admonished. "Have you lost your mind?"

"Tell him to take it back! I'm sick of him. I hate him!" Jordan screamed.

One of the deacons had the other little boy pinned down on the pew. His nose was bleeding and he was huffing heavily. "Don't nobody care 'bout you hating them. Don't nobody like you no way, stupid."

"I got yo' stupid!" Jordan tried to dive toward the boy again. Rachel caught him and pulled him back.

"Jordan!"

"Son, you need to settle down," Lester said, trying to take Jordan by the arm. Jordan snatched his arm away.

"Don't tell me what to do. You not my daddy!"

Rachel slapped Jordan upside the head. "Boy, what have I told you about saying that!" Even though he was close to Lester, lately, whenever Jordan got mad that was the first thing out of his mouth. Lester always took it pretty well, though; even now, he kept his calm demeanor.

Jordan was trying desperately to fight back tears. Rachel let out a long sigh as she dragged him away, mumbling an apology. She knew Lester would try to clean it up before finishing his sermon, but he might as well just dismiss church because no one would be listening.

Rachel ignored all the people staring at her and shaking their heads as she dragged Jordan down the aisle and out of the sanctuary.

"These kids today just ain't got no discipline," one longtime member muttered.

"They need to let me at him," an elderly lady said, "I'd beat some sense in him."

"Lord, Lord, Lord, this family is just full of drama," said another member, Sister Viola Smith.

Rachel rolled her eyes. She considered responding, but knew there wasn't much she could say because Sister Smith was right on the money. No matter how hard she tried, she just couldn't escape the drama.

chapter 2

Rachel paced back and forth across the living room of the massive six-thousand-square-foot house she'd called home for the last three months. She paused, glancing out the window at a car slowly making its way down her dead-end street. People were always coming into her gated community in Southwest Houston, gawking at the beautiful custom-built brick homes. It got on her nerves, especially right now. She chalked her irritation up to the fact that she was just angry right now and snapped back to her phone conversation.

"I'm telling you, Bobby, you need to get this boy under control before I have to hurt him!" She was squeezing the cordless phone so tightly against her ear, she thought she'd crack it.

Her son was locked in his bedroom upstairs. Rachel hated

calling on Bobby, but it was obvious she and Lester couldn't get through to Jordan's little bad behind.

"What do you want me to do, Rachel?" Bobby sounded exasperated, which was unusual because he always took an active interest in what was going on with Jordan.

"What do you mean, what do I want you to do? Be his daddy!"

"Every time I try, you won't let me. Need I remind you that just last month you told me, 'Lester's his daddy now.'"

Rachel sighed. She remembered that horrible conversation. As much as she tried to walk the straight and narrow, Bobby had a way of bringing out the ignorant side in her. Her best friend, Twyla, said it was because she was still in love with him. Rachel wouldn't even entertain that idea—it had taken her too long to get over Bobby. She definitely wasn't trying to backtrack.

"I apologized for that. You know I have no problem with you seeing Jordan."

"Yeah, when you feel like it. Even though we have joint custody, I can't ever get him until you say so."

"I'm just looking out for Jordan's best interests. You know how stupid your wife can get."

It was Bobby's turn to sigh. "Please don't start."

"Where is Mrs. Shante anyway? In the kitchen getting something to eat?" Like her sister, Shante was heavyset and Rachel had always taken pleasure in pointing that out even though she'd heard Shante had lost some weight.

Bobby hesitated. "Spoken like a true first lady, Rachel."

Rachel squeezed her eyes closed. Dangit, there she went again. She and Shante had history, from the time Rachel had tried to cut her with a five-inch blade to the time they'd gotten into a fight—on Shante and Bobby's wedding day. It had been nothing but bad blood between the two of them. That was a part of her life Rachel didn't care to revisit.

"Bobby, I'm sorry, that was uncalled for."

He let out a laugh. "Wow, I never thought I would live to see the day when Rachel Jackson apologized two times in one conversation."

A small smile crept up on Rachel's face. "Technically, that first time wasn't an apology. I was telling you I had apologized the *other* time."

"Two apologies in one lifetime is more than I ever thought I'd get." They both laughed at that. After the laughter died down a silence hung in the air. "I'll come get Jordan next weekend and have a talk with him, see if I can figure out why he's been acting up lately," Bobby offered.

Rachel sighed thankfully. She was at her wits' end with her son. He used to be a perfect angel; for the last six months he'd been a holy terror. "I appreciate that, Bobby. Lester has been trying to deal with him, but Jordan's being so disrespectful to him I'm gon' hurt him before it's all over. So whatever you can do, I appreciate it."

"No problem."

They were both silent again for a moment. Finally, Bobby spoke. "Rachel?"

"Yes?"

"What happened to us?"

Rachel almost dropped the phone. She definitely wasn't expecting him to go there. She'd always felt like Bobby was her soul mate, but she'd accepted a long time ago that what they'd had was gone for good. "Ummmm, wrong time, wrong place I guess," she replied as she got the phone situated back under her ear.

"Yeah, we were both young," Bobby replied wistfully. "If only . . ." He hesitated. "You know you will always be my one and only true love. You know that, right?"

Where is this coming from? She'd been crazy in love with Bobby, and had tried everything under the sun to get him back, yet nothing had ever worked. He'd broken her heart and married Shante. "Bobby, I . . . I don't know what to say." Rachel felt her heartbeat speeding up. *No, no, no,* she told herself. *You are so over him.*

"I'm unhappy, Rachel. Shante and I fight constantly. We're both miserable. I made a huge mistake marrying her." He sounded so pitiful.

"Bobby, you're just going through a hard time in your marriage. It's hard work." Rachel knew she should just hang up the phone but Bobby was her first love, not to mention her son's father. They'd broken up when she was eighteen after he went overseas to serve in the military and Rachel had gotten pregnant by his best friend, Tony, while he was gone. Even though Rachel had had a beautiful daughter, Nia, whom Bobby had come to adore, he was never able to get over Rachel's betrayal.

"I'm unhappy because I should have married you." Bobby rushed the words out.

Rachel was stunned. She would have given her right arm to hear those words seven years ago, when she showed up at Bobby's wedding and begged him not to marry Shante.

Now she weighed his declaration. Her heart wanted to tell him she would always love him, too. She felt her mouth forming the words when she looked up and saw Lester standing in the doorway. When had he gotten home from church?

"Honey, I just stopped by to pick up this book," he said, holding up Joel Osteen's latest. "It's for Sister Taylor. I'm running over there to pray with her. Her mother is very sick." Lester walked over and kissed Rachel on the head. "I love you. Don't worry about cooking. I'll stop and pick us up something on the way home. I just want you to relax. I'll talk to Jordan when I get back."

Rachel still had the phone to her ear as Lester walked out of the house. *The Lord will come just when the devil thinks he's winning.* Her mother's words of wisdom rang in her ears.

"Rachel, are you still there? Did you hear what I said?" Bobby asked.

Rachel stared at the phone before slamming it down and dropping to her knees. If ever she needed to pray for strength, it was now. She was a happily married woman and Bobby was the devil in disguise.

chapter 3

Angela Brooks stared at the legal document in disbelief. She read the heading for the twentieth time. "Petition for joint custody. Jonathan Edward Jackson versus Angela Brooks for minor child, Chase Antoine Brooks."

This could not possibly be happening. Jonathan could not possibly think that she would let their child live with him for any amount of time. Angela slumped to the floor in her two-bedroom condo. She had started a new life here in Atlanta. One far removed from the devastating lie she'd been living as Mrs. Jonathan Jackson. Married less than a month and pregnant with their child, she'd come home to discover that her perfect husband was far from perfect. After she overheard his conversation with his former lover, Jonathan admitted something she'd never in a million years thought she'd hear: He was gay. She'd been crushed and had moved away in shame.

Too stunned to cry, Angela reread the document. She couldn't make out all of the legal terms, but there was no doubt about it: This fool thought he was going to get her child on a regular basis.

Anger slowly took the place of disbelief and Angela pulled herself up off the floor. She stomped into her kitchen and snatched the cordless phone off its base. She looked up Jonathan's cell phone number in her Rolodex, which she only had because he was always sending her checks, checks she never cashed, and he always included his contact information as if she was really going to call. She punched in his number. He answered on the third ring.

"Have you lost your mind!" she screamed.

"Hello to you, too, Angela," Jonathan calmly replied.

"Skip the formalities, Jonathan. I got your funky little petition. You must be on that crack your brother is smoking if you think for one minute I'm going to let you have my child."

"First of all, David is clean, has been for several years now," Jonathan replied. "Second of all, Chase is my child, too. Angela, I never wanted it to come to this, but you won't even let me see him."

"See him for what? So you can teach him how to be a man?" she sneered.

"See him so I can let him know his father didn't abandon him." His calm tone was truly pissing her off.

"Oh, but that's where you're wrong. His father did abandon him when he chose a gay lifestyle."

"I didn't *choose* this lifestyle, Angela."

"Save the explanations, Jonathan. I told you before I'm not letting my child around you and your boyfriend." Angela stomped back and forth across her kitchen. She was so glad Chase was at school because she never wanted him to see her this angry.

"Angela, can we be civil, please?"

"Civil? You want civil? Let's see, I come home from shopping for our baby and I hear my new husband on the phone with his male lover talking about how much he misses him! I find out that my husband, the man I loved with all my heart, was using me to try to prove to himself that he was a 'real' man. You married me knowing you were gay! So you will have to excuse me if I don't feel very *civil*."

"It's been seven years."

"I don't care if it's been seventy years. That pain doesn't go away." In all those years, she'd never seriously dated again because she couldn't bring herself to trust a man. In fact, the few guys she had gone out with, she ended up dumping at the smallest sign of what she saw as "feminine" characteristics. She knew she was compulsive about it, but she couldn't help herself and eventually just resigned herself to a lifetime of being alone.

Jonathan let out a long sigh. "You're trying to punish me, but you're only hurting Chase by doing this."

"Look here, Jonathan. Your daddy might have forgotten what the Bible says about homosexuality, but I haven't.

Unh-unh. It ain't no turning the other cheek for me. And my child will not be exposed to your sinful lifestyle." Angela had prayed for months, begging God to help her understand why He would do this to her. She'd finally surmised that the devil had simply won the battle for Jonathan's soul and that God had abandoned her by letting her marry him in the first place.

"But I'm his father," Jonathan protested.

"And I'm his mother. And I will die before I ever let you have him!" Angela slammed the phone down. Jonathan didn't know who he was messing with. The old Angela was soft-spoken and wouldn't hurt a fly. But finding out your husband is gay can bring out the worst in you. And if Jonathan thought he was getting her child, he was definitely about to see the worst in her.

chapter 4

"Well, that went well," Jonathan mumbled as he closed his cell phone. He didn't know why he'd expected Angela to be reasonable.

"Come have a seat, son." Simon Jackson motioned toward the living room sofa across from him. "You knew it wasn't going to be easy."

Jonathan buried his face in his hands. He thought by coming out of the closet he would finally find happiness. And he had, for a little while. But now he was more depressed than he'd ever been; he knew it was because he missed his son.

"Dad, I deserve to be a part of my son's life."

"You hurt that girl, son," Simon replied matter-of-factly.

Jonathan lifted his head as his eyes watered. "I know,

Daddy. But how many ways can I say 'I'm sorry'? I can't help who I am."

Simon shifted uncomfortably in his recliner. Jonathan sighed. All this time and his father still wasn't comfortable with his lifestyle. They had reached an unspoken agreement years ago, that they just wouldn't address the issue. Sort of like don't ask, don't tell. Jonathan hated that he couldn't talk to his father about what he was feeling, but he knew his father wrestled with the issue himself on a daily basis. Simon caught flak from people who couldn't understand how a man of God could accept someone who was homosexual, but as he had told one of the deacons, "How do you just completely disown your own child, your own flesh and blood? I can't stand in judgment. He'll have to deal with God on that."

Coming to terms with his son's homosexuality had been a daily struggle for Simon, that much Jonathan knew. He looked like he'd aged two decades in the last few years. And Jonathan knew it was because of him. Simon's hair was now fully gray and he had bags under his eyes. The cancer had also taken its toll, robbing Simon of his youthful appearance and vibrant personality. He'd found out three years ago that he had prostate cancer. At first, he tried to hide it from his family and the church, but after the disease started affecting his ability to function normally, he'd broken down, told his family, and stepped down as pastor of Zion Hill. Although he was supposedly in remission, Simon was now only a shell of his former self. Jonathan also knew a huge part of his father's aging came from wrestling with his inner demons on accepting Jonathan's lifestyle. Jonathan had even heard him praying for God to deliver his son "from his gayness." If only it were that easy. Say a couple of Hail Marys and *poof!* you're no longer gay. Yeah, right. In the real world it just didn't work like that. People just didn't understand that if he'd had a choice, Jonathan would have chosen to live happily ever after with Angela.

After they split up, people kept asking why he'd married her in the first place. He never meant to hurt her. He really and truly thought he could make it work. He chuckled painfully. The sad part was he'd lost his marriage over Tracy and he and Tracy weren't even together anymore.

Tracy had gotten bored with the relationship two years into it and had taken off with a rich older man who was going to help him "find himself."

Now Jonathan's days were spent caring for his ailing father, working at an at-risk youth facility, and dreaming of his son.

"I have to see him. I have to be a part of his life," Jonathan said wistfully. Since the breakup with Angela, he'd only laid eyes on his son twice: once when he'd found out where Angela lived and had flown to Atlanta to spy on them for a few days and another time when he'd gotten word that she was visiting her parents here in Houston. He'd rented a car and staked out her parents' home until he saw them.

He'd sent money and short letters over the years to her, when he had her address, to her cousin, Melanie, when he didn't. Angela had never cashed the checks he'd sent, but she had sent him a photo of Chase when he turned three, along with a note that said, "Please leave us alone."

"I have gone too long without Chase in my life."

"But, son, you just have to take it slow." Simon coughed violently. Although it had been nearly eight years since his mother died, Jonathan couldn't bear the thought of losing his father as well.

Jonathan was just about to reply when the doorbell rang. He turned to his father. "I'll get it."

Jonathan walked over to the door and stared out the peephole. He quickly turned back to his father. "Dad, it's Sister Maylene. It looks like she's carrying a dish."

Simon sighed heavily. "Lord, you'd think the fact that I'm no longer head pastor would stop all these women from sniffing around here."

A smile crossed Jonathan's face. Ever since his mother died, his father had had little time for women. But it definitely wasn't from the women's lack of trying. Every time he turned around somebody was bringing by a sweet potato pie, or checking to see if Simon needed anything from the store, or just dropping by because they were "in the neighborhood."

"Dad, I think at some point, one of these women is going to break you down."

"Hmmph." Simon snorted.

"You want me to let her in?"

"Well, I guess since you got your eyeball all up in the peephole she knows we're in here. Let her in." Simon got up and walked into the kitchen. "I'll be in the back, trying to look busy."

Jonathan slowly opened the door. It was obvious Sister

Maylene was surprised to see him because the seductive look she had on her face quickly disappeared.

"Afternoon, Brother Jackson." She cleared her throat and tried to shift her purse in front of her, no doubt trying to hide the fact that she was exposing too much cleavage.

"How are you, Sister Maylene?" Jonathan asked, trying not to laugh. Her face was made up like she was twenty and she had taken down her signature bun; her white hair flowed freely down to her shoulders.

"Blessed and highly favored. Ummm, is ummm, is Pastor Jackson around?"

Jonathan stepped back and waved her in. "He's right in the kitchen," he said as he shut the door behind her.

She held out the covered dish. "Well, I was just bringing by supper for him since I know he's been a little under the weather."

"I can take it to him." Jonathan stuck his hands out, still trying not to laugh. He was so glad he'd come over here!

Sister Maylene quickly pulled the dish close to her chest. "Umm, I would much rather give it to him myself."

I bet you would, Jonathan thought. He stepped aside and motioned for her to pass.

"I'll only be a minute," she said as she sashayed past him.

"Sure." Jonathan could sense her disappointment as he followed her into the kitchen. It was obvious she didn't want him around.

Simon was at the kitchen table reading over some papers. He forced a smile when he looked up. "Sister Maylene, how are you today?"

"Just fine." She looked over at Jonathan like she was pleading with him to leave the room. Simon shot his son a look that Jonathan knew meant he should stay right where he was.

Jonathan sat down at the kitchen bar and he could've sworn Sister Maylene looked like she wanted to curse him out.

"Well, I know you don't get around much and I know it's not often you get a home-cooked meal, so I just wanted to bring you some of my special meat loaf," she said.

"Well, I sho' do appreciate it," Simon responded. He motioned for Jonathan to take the dish.

Miss Maylene stood like she was waiting on Simon to invite her to stay. "Well, I best get going," she said after he didn't.

Simon stood. "Let me see you out. It sure means a lot that you thought enough of me to bring me dinner."

She smiled as they walked out of the kitchen. Jonathan put the dish in the refrigerator while he waited for his father to return. A couple of minutes later Simon walked back in with a look of exasperation on his face.

"You know she really wanted to stay," Jonathan said.

"Boy, I don't have time for all these women. Just no shame, throwing themselves at a man. It's disgraceful." Simon gathered up his papers. "I'm going to take a nap."

Jonathan laughed as his father walked off. Simon would forever be comparing women to his wife, Loretta, who he always called the epitome of class.

Jonathan's laughter died down as he thought of his father spending the rest of his life alone. It was time for Simon to find someone to fill the void in his life. He paused as he thought about it. Was that what he was trying to do in attempting to win joint custody of his son?

He shook off the thought. The bottom line remained: He was Chase's father and he'd wasted enough time taking into account everyone else's feelings. Now the only person that mattered was Chase, and Jonathan wouldn't rest until he became a part of his son's life.

chapter 5

Lester rolled over, out of breath, his chest heaving. He had a look of absolute pleasure on his face. Poor thing, he really thought he'd done something, Rachel thought. But, as usual, his lovemaking left a lot to be desired.

Rachel exhaled as she looked at the digital clock on the nightstand. It was almost one in the morning and not only was she unfulfilled, she was still wide awake. She looked at Lester and a small smile crossed her face. He'd gone to sleep just that fast. He looked so peaceful. She, on the other hand, felt frustrated. She had resigned herself to a lifetime of mediocre loving, but it was starting to get to her. Oh, Lester tried, he tried with all his might, but he simply could not measure up to Bobby.

Rachel closed her eyes tightly. Why was she thinking of Bobby? He was history. He had chosen his life with his one-Reese's-Pieces-away-from-exploding wife, and she'd been forced to choose hers. Now that she was Mrs. Lester Adams, she could not backtrack with the man who had broken her heart.

But as Rachel looked over at her husband softly snoring she couldn't help but wonder, what if? What if she and Bobby had gotten back together? What if she had never cheated on him in the first place? What if she hadn't been so young and stupid? And why couldn't she get his words from the other day out of her head? *I'm unhappy because I should have married you.*

You need to pray, Rachel told herself as she climbed out of bed and dropped to her knees. Her mother would be thrilled to know that she had become a praying woman. It had helped her make it through some turbulent times. Back in the day, though, she had been a firecracker and had done some things she was now ashamed of.

Rachel prayed for a good five minutes before standing up and grabbing her robe. She felt a little better, but her thoughts were still on Bobby. Maybe if she went downstairs and watched TV, it would help her fall asleep—or at the very least get her mind off of Bobby.

As she made her way downstairs she couldn't help but recall all the horrible things she'd done during and after her relationship with Bobby. She shook her head as she thought about how she'd sent Jordan up to Bobby's door in the middle of the night. Or when she'd called and had all of Shante's utilities cut off. Or better yet, when she'd tried to stab Bobby with a

31

butcher knife. Rachel had worked hard to grow beyond that hot-tempered girl she used to be. But she couldn't help how she was feeling now.

When Bobby had left her, she couldn't understand why he wouldn't forgive her. It seemed stupid now. After all, she had a baby by his best friend. How many men could've forgiven that? But back then, she'd felt he was being unreasonable by not giving her another chance. And she especially couldn't understand why he chose overweight, plain-looking Shante over her.

Rachel knew she was pretty, always had been. But she'd let her hair grow out over the years and now it hung down on her shoulders. She'd also kept her svelte size-eight frame. Bobby used to love how guys were always looking at her. She used to think that and his love for her would be enough to win him back. But he'd made it clear that he loved Shante for what was on the inside, not how she looked.

It was a mature viewpoint that Rachel just hadn't understood at the time. Over the years, however, she'd grown up enough to do so. *So then why can't you stand Shante?* a little voice echoed in her head.

"Because I wish he'd chosen me," Rachel mumbled before quickly catching herself. "No, I don't. What am I talking about?"

"Ma, are you in here talking to yourself?"

Rachel jumped at the sound of Jordan's voice from behind her. She hadn't even realized she was standing in the kitchen, in the dark, talking to herself. She tried to fake a laugh. "I'm sorry, baby. I was just mumbling."

"Oh," Jordan muttered like he could really care less. "I just needed some water. I have the hiccups."

"Have a seat." Rachel walked over and flipped the light on. "I'll get you a glass of water. Maybe even make us some hot chocolate, and maybe we can chat for minute."

"Awww, Ma. I just want to get some water and go back to bed," he groaned.

Rachel ignored him as she grabbed a glass, filled it with water from the Ozarka machine, and placed it on the table. "Have a seat."

Jordan rolled his eyes as he plopped down at the table. Rachel grabbed two more cups from the cabinet, filled them with hot water and placed them in the microwave. After letting the water get hot, she removed the cups, filled them with cocoa, and placed them at the table.

"Here; now, let's talk," she said.

Jordan groaned again.

"You want to tell me what's going on with you?"

"Nothing, dang."

"Jordan, I don't like your attitude lately. You're rude and disrespectful, and I just don't understand what's going on with you."

Jordan sighed, then took a sip of his hot chocolate. "Why you trippin'?" he finally said.

"All right, don't get smart," she warned. "I'm just trying to get you to talk to me."

"What? Ain't nothing wrong. I wish everybody would just leave me alone!" Jordan scowled.

"Jordan, you're eleven. How bad can life really be?" Rachel tried to talk calmly because it was obvious something was wrong with her son. "Talk to me, please."

Jordan blew a frustrated breath, then sat up. "Fine. I wanna know why don't nobody like us. Why they're always talking about us. You, Uncle Jonathan, Uncle David, even Paw Paw Simon. Everybody hates us."

Rachel tried not to smile. She forgot that at his age, being liked was one of the most important things in the world. She put her hand on his. "Baby, nobody hates us."

"Yes they do. Everybody's always talking about us."

Rachel shook her head. "Sweetie, sometimes, when you're in a position of power, you're held to higher standards than everyone else. Your grandfather has always held a position of power, so people expected his kids to be perfect. But we had problems just like everybody else."

Jordan looked like he wasn't convinced.

"You know Sister Smith, Donyell's grandmother?" Rachel continued.

Jordan nodded. "What about her?"

"She's raising Donyell because his mother went to prison for bank robbery."

Jordan's eyes got wide as she kept talking.

"And Sister Hicks got arrested for shoplifting when she was a teenager."

"No way!"

"Yes way." Rachel smiled. "So, you see, everybody has issues. Some people act so holy that you think they've never done anything wrong—but no one on this earth is perfect."

Jordan looked like a huge weight had been lifted off his shoulders. Rachel was just grateful that he didn't ask her to go into details about her brothers. That was a conversation she wasn't ready to have with him just yet.

"Ma, can I ask you another question?"

"Of course you can."

He looked down and started fiddling with his fingers. "Why didn't you marry my daddy? I mean, I like Daddy Lester, but I'm just wondering."

Rachel sighed. "Baby, you know me, Lester, and your daddy all love you to death, right?"

"I know."

"Me and your father not marrying had nothing to do with you. I made a lot of mistakes when I was younger. And sometimes we hurt people so much that they can't forgive you." She was glad Jordan was too young to remember all the dirt she'd done, let alone the custody battle.

"So you hurt my daddy?"

Rachel didn't know how to answer that. She didn't want to lie. "Mommy did some things she's not proud of. You remember when you threw that baseball through Mrs. Logan's window on purpose because you were mad?"

He nodded.

"Well, after it was over, you regretted that. I did some things that I regretted, too. But know this: No matter what, you will always be the most important person in our lives. Understand?"

Jordan smiled for the first time in a long time. "Yeah, I understand." He took a sip of his cocoa, then stood up. "I'm gonna go back to bed."

Rachel stood and watched him head to the door. "Jordan?"

He stopped and turned around.

"No more problems at school, right? We straight?"

Jordan nodded. "Yeah, we straight."

Rachel turned out the kitchen light and watched her son make his way back to his room. He looked like such an angel. She hoped their conversation had gotten through to him and resolved whatever problem he was having. But for some reason, her gut was telling her her problems with Jordan were far from over.

chapter 6

Rachel wiped the sweat from her face. "Okay, boys and girls, take it from the top!" As one of the students hit the music to the song "Stomp" by Kirk Franklin, Rachel began counting the kids down. "Step, step, slap, step, slap, slap, turn around, slap."

She led them in the steps for a few minutes before stepping back and watching them finish the routine themselves in front of the church sanctuary. She had more than twenty kids on the step team and all of them were at practice tonight. She wished she could get Jordan to participate, but—of course—he had no interest in doing anything church related.

Rachel smiled as the stepping calmed down and a young man with cornrows took the mike off the podium.

"Give it up! Give it up! Give it up for my G-O-D!" He then

proceeded to rap while the steppers behind him clapped along. "I'm shooting straight from the hip and it's plain to see. Can't nobody mess with the power of my G-O-D."

"Good God Almighty."

Rachel turned toward the four church members standing in the back of the sanctuary.

"Is he rapping about God?" mumbled Birdie Mae Canton, one of the deacons' wives. She had a look of absolute horror on her face.

"What has this world come to?" her cohort, Norma Jean Woodruff, asked as she clutched her chest.

Birdie Mae stomped to the front. She looked twenty years older than she actually was. It was probably the flowered dress that hung on her robust frame. Or maybe it was the hair, which was pulled back so tightly in a bun that it slanted her eyes. "Sister Adams, please tell me what is going on," she spat.

"What does it look like?" Rachel responded in as nice a voice as she could muster. She motioned for the kids to keep going.

The boy continued to rap. "If you feeling God like I'm feeling God, let me hear you say, 'oh yeah.'"

"Oh yeah!" the kids behind him shouted.

All four women continued to stand with their mouths open. "It looks like these chilluns done lost their mind." Birdie Mae spun on them and clapped her hands together. "Stop it! Stop that rapping, stepping, and blasphemous noise!"

Rachel took a deep breath. "This is our new step team, Sister Canton."

"Step team? What do we need a step team for? This is church, not some fraternity," Norma Jean interjected.

"I know that, but I told you one of my goals was to make this congregation more appealing to young people. And I'm sorry, but this is what young people like."

"Rapping? Stepping? In God's name? You think that's okay?" Birdie Mae asked in disbelief.

"I sure do." Rachel turned back to the kids. "Okay, one more time from the top."

The kids looked nervously at Birdie Mae. She taught many of them in Sunday school, so Rachel was sure they were nervous about proceeding against her wishes.

Birdie Mae shot the kids a mean look before turning back to Rachel. "Sister Adams, we stood by and watched as you came in here and cut out the announcements, cut out the devotionals and the testimonies, in an effort to, may I quote, 'cut the service time.' Heaven forbid we should give the Lord more than two hours on Sunday morning. Then we stood by and watched as you started some youth group bringing in wayward girls from off the streets. We even allowed you to unnecessarily bring in a huge band to accompany our already talented choir."

Norma Jean leaned in. "And don't forget about her getting rid of the choir robes. Got everybody looking all mismatched."

Birdie Mae nodded. "Of course. And let's not even get started on the drama ministry, as if we need to act out a show for God. You did all of that with little protest from us, but this is going too far. I, for one, will not stand by and let you desecrate this church. Your mother would never have done something like this. Not only are you setting a horrible example for young people, but you are not honoring God with this nonsense. No, this will not happen."

Rachel had had enough. This was exactly why she didn't want to be first lady; technically, she should be able to handle this situation with style and grace. But she wasn't feeling very graceful right about now.

"Look here, Birdie Mae, I ain't my mama. That's number one. Number two, there's a new sheriff in town. And I do things differently." Rachel calmed herself down before continuing. "As first lady, I am in charge of the church program and our youth. And I say the program was too long and our youth are too bored. So we will step, dance, rap, act, and whatever else it takes to get them involved. And if you don't like it, well, let's just say Mount Calvary is always looking for new members."

Birdie Mae clutched her chest. "I have been a tithing member of this church for thirty-two years!"

"And I have been first lady for one. While we appreciate your years of service, if you can't respect our changes . . . well, that's just too bad." Rachel didn't give her time to respond. She turned back to the children. "Okay, Joseph, that was a good rap. Let's try it again with a little more energy."

She ignored Birdie Mae and her flunkies as they stomped out of the church, mumbling what Rachel was sure was a mouthful of threats.

chapter 7

Angela toyed with her now-cold coffee. She hadn't been able to think straight for the past week, ever since she'd gotten Jonathan's outrageous demand that he have joint custody.

"So, girl, what you gon' do?"

Angela's head jerked up. She was so engrossed in her own problems, she forgot she was sitting here with her girlfriend, Constance. They were at Starbucks in Buckhead for their standard Saturday morning meeting.

"Huh?" Angela responded.

"I said, what are you gonna do? I mean he *is* Chase's father," Constance said.

"I don't care," Angela said, bringing her attention back to

her conversation. "I am not about to let my child be around my homosexual ex and his boyfriend."

"Or girlfriend." Constance giggled.

Angela eyed her high-school friend. "Ain't nothing funny about this, Constance." Constance was her girl, but she could be so insensitive. Still, Angela was grateful to her. She'd opened her home to Angela after the whole fiasco with Jonathan. Angela had initially moved to Wisconsin, but Constance had convinced her there was nothing for her there and persuaded her to come to the "Mecca" city of Atlanta.

"Chill out, girl," Constance replied. "I'm just trying to cheer you up."

"I can't be cheered up, especially if that bastard thinks he's coming anywhere near my child." Angela sipped her coffee and grimaced as the cold coffee slid down her throat.

Constance hesitated, then said, "I'm going to ask this—and don't get mad or anything—but you don't think that man has a right to see his child?"

"He doesn't have any rights as far as I'm concerned."

Constance was just about to say something when a huge grin crossed her face. "Umph, umph, umph, look who's walking this way."

Angela turned and grimaced at the sight of the tall chocolate man with the broad shoulders approaching them.

"Well, if it isn't my two favorite women," he said.

"Hey, Lance," Constance said sweetly.

"Hey, Constance." He turned his attention to Angela. "Angela, how are you today?"

"Fine, just in the middle of something here." She glared at Constance, who was kicking her under the table.

Lance looked a little disappointed. "Oh, well, I won't hold you. I just wanted to say hello." He started walking off but stopped and looked at Angela. "You know, the dinner invitation is still open."

Angela nodded. "I'll keep that in mind."

Lance stood in awkward silence for a few seconds before waving good-bye and continuing on to get his coffee.

As soon as he walked off, Constance leaned in. "You think you can be just a little more rude?"

"What?" Angela said, frowning.

"First of all, you are a beautiful caramel queen who looks like she should've been a model in another life. And that man is only the finest specimen on the face of the earth. He has a great job, benefits, and a Benz. And as his personal banker, I can tell you he's never bounced a check. You can't beat that." Constance shook her head as she took a swig of her coffee. "How long has he been trying to get you to go out now?"

Angela groaned. "About six months."

"And explain to me why you won't go out with him?"

"That's just not where my head is at," Angela said.

Constance threw her hands up. "You and this vow of celibacy 'bout to get on my nerves. It's one thing if you were doing it for religious reasons, but the only reason you're doing it is because you're mad at all men."

"I just don't want to date right now, all right? Besides, he's too pretty. He's tall and pretty like Jonathan," Angela added, recalling Jonathan's soft features, flawless light brown skin, and almost-perfect body. Angela eyed Lance at the counter. "And he's dressed like he just stepped off the pages of *GQ*. Anybody that puts that much time into his appearance has got to be on the DL."

Constance lost her smile as she stared at her friend. "You've got to stop looking for signs of homosexuality in every man you meet."

"Whatever, Constance."

After a few more minutes of silence, Constance spoke up. "Have you given any thought to what you'll do if the judge orders you to let Jon see Chase?"

Angela shook her head. The thought was just too difficult to even consider. "I will just become one of those women on the run like you see on Lifetime."

"Come on, you know that's not the answer."

"Then what is, Constance? And don't tell me to compromise and allow Jonathan visitation. Him getting anywhere near my child is not an option!" Angela was serious about that. And nobody was going to convince her otherwise.

"Have you talked to Pastor Hayes?" Constance asked.

Angela rolled her eyes. She wasn't the faithful churchgoer she used to be. Since God had allowed her to marry and conceive a child with a gay man, her faith had evaporated. "You know he's gon' give me that whole forgiveness speech and I'm not hearing that."

"Well, do you really think you should be moving back to Houston, then?"

Angela weighed her friend's words. That had to be why Jon was making this custody demand. He must have found out she was moving home. "Trust me, I've thought of that," she replied. "But I've already sold my house here. The people who bought it close next week and I start my new job in Houston on the first."

"Yeah, but you can get another house and another job here," Constance protested.

"Believe me, I've played out all the possibilities. But the company already paid my moving expenses and I bought a new place. If I renege on the job, I have to pay all that money back and you and I both know I don't have it like that."

"Yeah, I feel you. I just know being back there will only make Jonathan want to see Chase more."

"Constance, read my lips: That punk isn't getting anywhere near my child. *Comprende?*"

Constance threw up her hands. "Hey, I'm with you. I hope they never let Chase around Jonathan. But I was just saying, be prepared in case they do."

"Oh, believe me, I have a few tricks up my sleeve. See, I disappeared into the sunset the weak, heartbroken wife. But I'm returning a different woman. And believe me when I tell you Jonathan Jackson won't like the new me."

chapter 8

Jonathan eased open the front door of his father's house. He spent so much time here, he might as well move in. With his brother David living here, though, and showing no signs of leaving any time soon, that was out of the question. Besides, it probably was best that David was still at home since their dad was so sick all the time. Jonathan relished the peace of his two-bedroom condo anyway.

Jonathan walked down the hallway adorned with photos of him, David, and Rachel at different phases in their lives. He stopped and fingered one of his mother holding Rachel. He and David were standing behind her. Jonathan felt his eyes mist up. How he wished his mother was here. If anybody could get through to Angela, she could.

"I love you, Mama," he whispered before he continued into the den. David was stretched out across the sofa, deeply engrossed in a telephone conversation. Jonathan could tell his brother was getting frazzled, which meant he was most likely talking to his ex-girlfriend, Tawny. Jonathan knew David struggled each day to stay free of drugs and couldn't help but worry that he would have a relapse fooling with Tawny.

David had been doing well since he went cold turkey right after their mother died. It was a promise he'd made to his mother and he'd worked to fulfill that promise, even breaking it off with Tawny. He'd gotten a maintenance job at the YMCA and had worked his way up to his current position as assistant director of boys' programs. Then Tawny had shown up out of the blue a couple of months ago and he'd been in a foul mood ever since.

"Listen to me, Tawny!" David yelled as he sat up on the sofa. "I do not believe you. This is just another one of your hustles. Quit calling me. I'm not gon' tell you again, just lose my number!" He slammed the phone down.

"Dang, what was that about?" Jonathan asked, finally walking into the room.

"Nothing, man, nothing," David replied, obviously flustered.

Jonathan studied his brother. David had been heading to the NFL until he tore his anterior cruciate ligament (ACL) his sophomore year of college and had had to give up football. He ended up dropping out of college, working off and on for the state until he was injured again while trying to hang lights for a Christmas function. He'd stayed on disability for what seemed like forever. Then he'd hooked up with Tawny and his life just went from bad to worse. He'd almost overdosed a couple of times and had been to rehab more times than Jonathan could count. No matter what, David couldn't get that crack monkey off his back—until their mother died. That had been the catalyst to get David to turn his life around. Jonathan hoped his brother wasn't having a relapse.

"You all right?" he asked, his voice laced with concern.

"Yeah, I'm fine. Now just get off my back, please."

"Don't bite my head off," Jonathan said as he sat down in the recliner across from his brother. "You just seem a little upset, that's all."

"I'm straight. Tawny's trippin'. I swear, I don't know what I ever saw in that girl." David took a deep breath. "What's up with you? You hear back from Angela yet?"

Jonathan's mood immediately changed. "Yeah, she went clean off on me."

David laughed as he relaxed a bit. "What, sweet little Angela?" He seemed to enjoy the break from whatever was stressing him out about Tawny.

"Yeah." Jonathan nodded. "The woman I talked to on the phone sounded anything but sweet."

David flashed a sly smile. "Well, I guess finding out your man is on the down low can do that to you."

Jonathan sighed. He was so sick of people making those little sarcastic comments. "Come on, that was seven years ago."

"And?"

"And, I'm no longer on the DL," Jonathan huffed.

"Yeah, that's right, you're all the way out." David snickered. "By the way, have you talked to your man?"

Jonathan rolled his eyes at his brother. By now he should've been used to David's remarks, but they still bothered him. "No, I haven't talked to Tracy in six months. He's moved on. And so have I." Jonathan stood up and walked over to the window to stare outside.

"Tell that to someone who doesn't know you. Tracy might have moved on, but you sure haven't. Tell me this, lil' bro, do you have any regrets?" David propped his feet up on the coffee table.

Jonathan debated giving his brother the standard "everything's fine" answer, but he had been waiting for an opportunity to bare his soul. "I have plenty of regrets. I regret taking that call from Tracy and causing Angela to walk out of my life."

"Why?"

"I . . . I don't know. My child is not a part of my life. I gave up my life with Angela, and me and Tracy didn't even work out." Jonathan tried to laugh, but he couldn't help but note how pathetic it sounded.

"But if you stayed with Angela, you wouldn't have been happy."

Jonathan thought about it. David was right. That was how he got in the situation with Angela in the first place. He'd married her trying to pretend that he was something he wasn't and in the end it had blown up in his face.

"Why don't you find someone else?"

"That's not even on my mind right now." Jonathan huffed. "Look, can we change the subject? I need to figure out how I'm going to handle this."

"Handle what?" Rachel asked as she walked into the den. She plopped down on the sofa next to David.

"I didn't hear you come in," Jonathan said.

"I used my key," Rachel responded as she held up her key ring.

"Does everyone still have a key?" David asked.

"Look, at least we're not mooching off of Daddy." Rachel pushed her brother's shoulder. Jonathan smiled at their playful banter. It reminded him of when they were all little, fussing, fighting, and driving their parents crazy.

"Where's Dad?" Rachel asked, looking around.

"Where else? Somebody's church." David laughed.

"Sick and all, some things never change." Rachel looked at Jonathan. "What's going on with you, Jonathan?"

"He's finally trying to make a move and see his son," David responded.

"What?" Rachel smiled. "You're finally listening to your little sister. I told you a long time ago you needed to try and get visitation. It's only fair."

Jonathan shrugged. "I just know how much I hurt Angela and I didn't want to cause her any more grief."

"Look, who you sleep with should have no bearing on whether you're capable of raising your child," Rachel said. "By the way, doesn't he have a birthday coming up?"

"Yep, he'll be seven." Jonathan's mood darkened. "I've missed seven years of his life. I just can't do it anymore."

"And you shouldn't," Rachel said as she got up and walked over to her brother. She took his hand and squeezed it. "Angela will just have to get over it. Is she still moving here?"

"As far as I know," Jonathan responded. "We have court in two weeks. My attorney said I have a good shot because the case is going before a pretty liberal judge."

"You want us there?" Rachel asked.

"That would mean the world to me." Jonathan smiled as he looked at his siblings. Growing up, they had never been close. David had been jealous because their father had always doted on Jonathan and didn't hesitate to let them know he felt Jonathan was the favorite son. David had resented it throughout their childhood. And Rachel had always been so lost in her own, spoiled little world. Then, of course, they'd all resented their father not ever having time for any of them. But their mother always used to say God works in mysterious ways. Her death had brought them all closer.

"Well, you know, any dirty little trick Angela thinks she can pull, I've been there, done that. So she can't come here thinking she's going to get over," Rachel warned.

"No, Angela's not like that. She's not the type to play dirty," Jonathan said. He stopped and frowned. "Or at least she didn't used to be. I don't know anymore. But still, I don't want this thing to get ugly."

"Please," Rachel replied. "Ain't nothing like a woman

scorned—trust me when I tell you, I doubt very seriously if Angela is the same sweet woman you remember."

Jonathan weighed his sister's words. Something in his gut told him Rachel was right on the money. He was in for the fight of his life.

chapter 9

Rachel stood in the doorway of Lester's office and stared at her husband and the floozy leaning over him with her double Ds all up in his face. *Why did these people insist on making me regress?* She was trying to be good and upstanding, but when tramps like nasty Nikki Rollins continued to get all up in her husband's face, it was just plain difficult. Lester was sitting at his desk pointing something out to Nikki on a piece of paper. She was giggling like a schoolgirl.

"Pastor, you are so smart," Nikki said as she leaned in closer. "I never would've figured that out."

"You want to get those things up out of my husband's face?" Rachel said through clenched teeth as she stomped into the office.

Lester immediately stood up. "Hi honey. I . . . I was just

helping Nikki get a better understanding of the Scripture she plans to teach in Sunday school," he said nervously, probably because he knew things were about to get ugly.

Rachel strutted into the room, keeping her eye on Nikki, who was now standing up straight trying to look innocent. "Oh, she's gon' need some help all right. She's gon' need help putting her weave back in because I'm about two seconds from snatching it out of her head."

"Sister Adams . . . I . . . I wasn't doing anything," Nikki stammered as she ran her fingers through her two-tone burgundy hair.

"Not from lack of trying!" Rachel said, motioning toward the breasts that looked like they were screaming to get out of Nikki's low-cut blouse. "You need to take your trashy behind back to Sweet Poke, Salt Lick, or whatever the name of that country town is you blew in from because you don't know who you messing with."

"Rachel!" Lester admonished.

Rachel spun toward her husband. "What?"

"What are you doing?" Lester looked like he was pleading with his eyes for her to calm down.

Rachel's nostrils flared. "I'm informing Sister Rollins that she's flirting with the wrong woman's husband." Back in the day, Rachel wouldn't have hesitated to throw down, but she was older now. And a first lady. And trying to do better in her walk with God. But at the same time, she had to let these women know she wasn't her mama. Loretta Jackson used to turn the other cheek to these floozies and just trust that "God will keep my husband faithful," as she always used to say. Well, Rachel was gonna give God a little help. Plus, she simply could not allow herself to be disrespected the same way those women had disrespected her mother.

Lester was frazzled. He turned toward Nikki. "Sister Rollins, please excuse us. I need a word with my wife."

Nikki scurried out of the room. She had barely closed the door when Lester took a deep breath and motioned to the chair in front of his desk. "Sit down."

Rachel stood with her arms crossed, a defiant look on her face.

Lester sighed. "Sit down. Please."

Rachel kept her lips poked out as she sat down.

"Rachel, I have asked you time and time again to please refrain from going off on the women of the church," Lester said as he sat down behind his desk.

"And I have asked you time and time again to keep these tramps up out of your face." Rachel crossed her legs as she glared at her husband.

"Rachel, you're being unreasonable. Part of my job as minister is to counsel and advise members of the congregation, and that includes female members."

Rachel stared at her husband. He was making her sick. He was like her father, too blind to see that these women were after one thing and one thing only—to take her spot as first lady. "Lester, Nikki was all over you." She tried to speak calmly. "For a minute I thought she was trying to breastfeed you."

"Don't be ridiculous."

"Don't be naive."

"Rachel, I'm tired of having this conversation with you over and over. Last month, you went off on Veronica Melborne because you said she was staring at my behind."

"Well, she was," Rachel said, cutting him off.

Lester held up his hand. "Let me finish. The month before that, you got upset at the women on the auxiliary board because you said they were talking about you and how I could do so much better."

"Well, they were. And you can't."

"This is crazy," Lester huffed. "You know I love you and only you. This insane, petty jealousy has got to stop. When are you going to grow up?"

Rachel stared at him like he had lost his mind. "Grow up? Grow up? Oh, so now I'm immature?" That was a slap in the face, considering how hard she had been working at being a "mature and responsible" first lady.

"Rachel, you're putting words in my mouth," he sighed.

"Words in your mouth? Your exact words were 'when are you going to grow up.'"

"I didn't mean it like that."

"Just how did you mean it, then, Reverend Adams?"

"I meant to say . . . oh, forget it." He shook his head.

Rachel uncrossed her legs and scooted to the edge of the chair. "No, let's not forget it."

"Rachel, I have a sermon to prepare for. I'm not going to go through this with you." He flicked his hand, turned his back, and began typing on his computer.

"Did you just dismiss me?" Rachel stared at him in disbelief. Lester buried his face in his hands. Rachel reached out and knocked all of the papers off his desk. "You are crazy if you think you can just dismiss me!"

Someone knocked at the door. Lester seemed relieved by the interruption as he turned around in his seat. "Yes, come in."

Deacon Bishop Long stuck his head in the door. "Pastor, the people are here to install the new organ. They need you to tell them where you want it."

Lester immediately jumped up. "Tell them I'll be right out." He turned his attention back to Rachel. "I'll be here late tonight because we have a finance meeting. Do you want me to pick the kids up from your dad's?"

Rachel debated continuing the argument, but she was tired herself and right about now she couldn't stand the sight of her husband. "Naw, they're spending the night."

"Well, do you want to go catch a late movie or something? I'll be out of here around nine." He looked like he desperately wanted to let their argument slide.

"You know what, don't worry about it. I'm sure Nikki will need some more counseling or help with her Sunday school lesson or something. I know how important that is to you, so you just stay here and do that. Don't bother rushing home because I'm going out." Rachel grabbed her purse and headed for the door. These people at Zion Hill better realize that she was not about to be pushed around, not even by her husband.

chapter 10

Twyla Huff stood with her mouth open. The music thumped throughout the dark building, the bass sounds reverberating across the room. Sweaty bodies were grinding against one another on the crowded dance floor.

Rachel turned to her friend. "What?"

"I'm just trying to figure out what you're doing," Twyla yelled so Rachel could hear her over the music.

Rachel ignored her and turned back to the bar. "I'm having a good time. What does it look like I'm doing?" She bobbed her head up and down to the sounds of music she didn't even recognize, let alone understand.

Luckily, the deejay switched to a slow song so they didn't have to shout to hear one another anymore. "Number one, you are not having a good time. Number two, you haven't been to a club in over a year," Twyla said as she tried to reason with Rachel.

Rachel eased her glass up to her mouth as she took a seat at the bar. Surprisingly, she hadn't really had a desire to go out in the last year because she'd been so busy at church, but Lester had really pissed her off tonight. "I would say that just means I'm overdue," she said as she sipped her drink.

"And you're drinking at that!" Twyla shook her head in disbelief.

"So? There's wine in the Bible and there is nothing wrong with a little glass of white Zinfandel."

"Well, I know I don't know much about the Word, but I don't think anybody in the Bible had their wine while they were up in Visions listening to Lil Jon and the Eastside Boyz."

"Twyla, I asked you to come along so we could just hang out and have a good time, just like we used to do back in the day," Rachel said.

"That's just it—that was back in the day." Twyla scrunched up her face as the music got louder and some rapper started spouting more words no one could understand. "We are older and I like to think wiser. I'm a freaking schoolteacher. I might see some of my students in here. And let's not even mention what the deacon board would say about you being here."

Rachel spun around on her bar stool and pointed a finger at Twyla. "See, that's what you don't get. I don't care what the deacon board, Reverend Adams, Reverend Jackson, or any of them other hypocrites at that church say about what I do."

Rachel was fed up. Since she'd become first lady, she had tried to change, tried to become who they all wanted her to be. And she still couldn't get any respect. "Screw them. I'm gon' be me and see how they all like that."

Twyla was about to say something but stopped when a man with gold across his whole top row of teeth stepped up to them at the bar. He was wearing a shiny purple suit with matching purple gators.

"Ummmph, ummphh, umphh. Dang girl, you look like Natalie Cole," he said as he stepped toward Twyla.

Twyla looked confused. "Natalie Cole?"

"Yeah, girl. Unforgettable," he said with a wide grin, displaying his teeth.

Rachel giggled. Twyla looked like she wanted to throw up. She took a deep breath. "Look, Luther—"

It was the man's turn to look confused. "Hey, how do you know my name?"

Twyla turned up her nose again. "It's plastered across your teeth."

The man touched his mouth and laughed. "Oh yeah, right, right."

Rachel leaned in to look at his grill, which he proudly displayed.

"Yep, it says Luther right across the front." Rachel tried not to crack a smile. "Bet that set you back a pretty penny."

"Sho' did," he said. "But it ain't nothing but a thang. I got money to burn, baby." He turned toward Twyla and licked his lips. "And I sho' would like to set you on fire with some of it."

Rachel was just about to comment when she noticed the leggy girl with the blonde braids standing behind Luther.

"I know you ain't up in this club all over some other skank!"

Luther spun around. "Michel'le!" He looked like he had the fear of God in him. "I . . . I thought you weren't coming."

"I bet you did," the woman said, pushing him out of the way. "Who is this tramp?" she asked, pointing at Twyla. She didn't give Twyla time to answer as she stepped toward her. "I know you not trying to step to my man. 'Cause I will cut your bourgeois behind like my name is Jack the Ripper."

Twyla looked terrified. Luther grabbed Michel'le by the arm. "Come on, baby. It ain't even like that."

"Then what it's like, Luther, huh, fool?" She snatched her arm away. "I saw you all up in her face!"

Luther tried to rub her braids. "Babe, chill. She was telling me she got some Louis Vuittons for sale in her car and was asking me did I want some. You know it's loud in here, that's why I was leaning up on her. I was trying to figure out which one I wanted to get you."

Michel'le looked at him like she was trying to decide if he was telling the truth. "For real, Luther? You bet' not be lying to me."

He stepped in and put his arms around her waist. "Girl, you know I ain't lying to you. Come to think of it, I don't even want to buy my baby no knockoffs. I'm gon' take you to the Galleria tomorrow and get you the real thing."

Michel'le squealed in delight. Luther turned to Twyla, his

arm draped around Michel'le's neck. "Sorry, but I'm gon' have to pass on the bags. My baby deserves the real thang." Michel'le planted a kiss on Luther's cheek as they strutted off into the corner.

"If that isn't enough to convince you it's time to go, I don't know what is," Twyla said, turning to Rachel. "So, please can we get out of here?"

Rachel looked around the club. Besides that little entertaining episode, she really wasn't having a good time. She used to keep the clubs hot in her younger days. But now she felt totally out of her element. She looked at her watch. It was almost midnight. Lester should be home by now; he was probably wondering where she was. She'd intended to stay out till two or three and really make him mad, but she felt her body wearing down.

"All right. Fine. Let's go." Rachel opened her purse, pulled out two twenties, and slid them toward the bartender. "Here, this is for our tab. Keep the change."

Rachel caught up with Twyla, who had already walked to the other side of the dance floor. "Would you wait up?"

"I am ready to go *now*," Twyla repeated.

Rachel grabbed Twyla's arm and turned her toward the dance floor. "Look. Is that who I think it is?"

Twyla peered at the dance floor. "Bobby?" She looked at Rachel suspiciously. "You knew he was going to be here, didn't you?"

"I swear I didn't." Rachel quickly pulled out a mirror and checked her makeup. No, she didn't want Bobby anymore, but she still wanted to look good whenever he saw her. "I'll be right back."

Rachel ignored Twyla's protests as she strutted over to the dance floor. Bobby was dancing with some woman who looked old enough to be his mother. Rachel pretended she didn't see him as she stopped and started talking to some man she had no interest in.

She looked out of the corner of her eye and caught Bobby staring at her. He whispered something to the woman he was with and then walked over to Rachel.

"What's up, Rachel?" Bobby said.

Rachel feigned surprise. "Hey, Bobby. How are you?"

The guy Rachel had been talking to looked back and forth between Rachel and Bobby.

"Yo, man, can you excuse us for a minute?" Bobby said.

The man looked like he was about to protest, but Rachel smiled. "I'll see you around."

He frowned before walking off.

Rachel turned back to Bobby, a big smile plastered across her face. He looked so good in his black leather jacket, black T-shirt, and black slacks. His sandy brown hair and gray eyes, even his cleft chin, were as sexy as ever. It was amazing how much Jordan looked like him.

"What are you doing here?" Bobby asked. His tone definitely was not what she expected. Usually, it would have been condescending, like she was doing something wrong. But this time he actually sounded pleasantly surprised to see her.

"The same thing you are, getting my groove on."

"Do you really think you should be out in a club?"

"Now, Bobby, you know me well enough to know I don't do things the traditional way."

"Where's your husband?"

"Where's your wife?" she responded pointedly.

He ignored her. "You do know the good reverend is going to go off when he finds out his wife went to a club."

"You do know I could care less about him going off."

A small smile finally crept up on Bobby's face. "Hmmmm, trouble in paradise?"

"You'd love that, wouldn't you?" Rachel knew she had put on her flirtatious voice, but she couldn't help it. Bobby just brought out the bad girl in her.

"How's my son?" he asked.

"You still coming to get him this weekend?"

"Yeah, I'm taking him to the Rockets game."

"Make sure you talk to him again about his behavior. Whatever you said last time didn't work," Rachel said as she recalled the two notes that had been sent home from his teacher this week. She'd decided that there was nothing emotionally wrong with Jordan. He was just being bad.

"I'll do that. You can drop him off at any time. Shante moved out. She and I are getting a divorce."

Rachel didn't know whether to shout for joy or cry. She had envisioned this day for years. But now that she'd settled into a quiet existence with Lester, it was not the news she wanted to hear.

Bobby stared at Rachel and she could tell he was taking a trip down memory lane. "Dang, girl, you look good."

Rachel blushed. The confidence she'd had just minutes ago was gone. She felt her heart start beating fast.

Just then Twyla came over to her. "Hey Bobby," she said, before turning to Rachel. "Can we please go now? These people here are getting on my nerves and all this rap is making my head hurt. You—"

Twyla stopped talking mid-sentence and looked back and forth between Rachel and Bobby, who were staring at each other like they were the only two people in the room. Twyla cleared her throat. "Excuse me, anybody notice me standing here?"

Both of them snapped out of their daze. "Oh, what's up, Twyla, where's James?" Bobby said, referring to Twyla's husband and Bobby's first cousin.

"He's at home and he's going to kill me if I don't get there soon," she said, turning her attention back to Rachel.

"Oh, okay," Rachel said. "I guess we should be going." She kept her gaze on Bobby.

"How'd you all get here?" Bobby asked.

"I drove," Twyla said as she shot Rachel another look. "And I'm about to leave, with or without you."

"Hey, look here, Twyla, ummm, why don't you go on home? I'll drop Rachel off. I wanted to go to IHOP or something 'cause I had some stuff I needed to talk to her about."

Twyla looked at him like he was crazy. "Some stuff like what?" she asked.

"About Jordan," Bobby replied.

Rachel was speechless. Flirting with Bobby over the phone or in a place filled with hundreds of people was one thing, but to be in a car alone with him, just the two of them, was something totally different. Suddenly the reality of what she was doing set in. Lester was a good man. She'd left her wild ways behind her. *Well, then what are you doing up in the club?* the little nagging voice in her head asked.

"Ummm, it's . . . it's getting late. Twyla's right. I better get going," Rachel stammered.

Bobby looked disappointed. "Are you sure? I, um, I'd really like to talk to you."

It took every ounce of strength in her body, but Rachel took a deep breath and replied, "Yeah, I'm sure. Just give me a call, okay? We'll talk later."

She grabbed Twyla's arm and pulled her out of the club. Rachel didn't stop until they were inside the car. She closed her eyes and leaned her head back against the seat.

"You want to tell me what that was about?" Twyla said as she started the car.

"That," Rachel said as she opened her eyes and looked at her friend, "is what they mean when they say the devil is always hard at work."

chapter 11

Lester opened the refrigerator, pulled out the orange juice, poured a glass, then put the carton back in the refrigerator. He walked over to the toaster and dropped a piece of bread in. He stood there waiting on it to brown. When it popped up, he snatched it out, grabbed a paper towel and sat down at the kitchen table and began nibbling on his toast.

Rachel sat across from him at the table. "So, you're just not going to say anything to me all morning," she said, staring at him.

Lester didn't respond and just kept chewing.

"Lester, I said I was sorry for staying out so late." Rachel had tried to stay mad, but his refusal to even talk to her when she finally made it in last night and told him where she'd been had caused her to break down and apologize.

Lester finally stopped chewing and glared at her. "A club. My wife, the first lady of one of the best churches in Houston, was up in a nightclub, doing God knows what, with God knows who."

Rachel rolled her eyes. She should've just lied when she came in last night. But Lester was waiting up and she felt bad enough about the conflicted emotions running through her mind over Bobby that she'd told him she'd gone out to Visions.

"I wasn't doing anything but hanging out," Rachel said.

"Hanging out? You're dang near thirty years old, why do you still feel the need to hang out?" Lester was furious. Rachel couldn't recall the last time she'd seen him so angry.

"I won't be thirty for three more years. And you say that like thirty is old or something anyway. That's crazy! I'm still young and if I want to go out and have a good time now and then, I don't see the problem with that."

"You don't see the problem?" He got up and started pacing across the kitchen. "We lead by example, Rachel! How am I supposed to get up and preach to people about how wrong it is to be hanging out in clubs until all hours of the night when you're doing that very thing?"

This argument was starting to get on her nerves, especially since Lester was starting to sound just like her father: always worried about what the people of Zion Hill would think. "I don't care how or what you preach. You got the calling. I didn't. I try to be supportive of you and that church, but you can't even respect me enough to stop these tramps from getting all up in your face, so why should I respect you enough to stay out of the club?"

"So this is all about Nikki, isn't it?"

Rachel glared at him. "Hell, yeah, it's about Nikki!"

"Rachel, I have asked you over and over, please do not curse."

"Oh, give me a break! 'Hell' is not a curse word. Heaven or hell, remember?"

"That is not the context in which you used the word."

"Whatever, Lester." She rolled her eyes.

Lester stared at Rachel. "You are being ridiculous. I need you to grow up and start acting like a proper first lady."

"And how does a proper first lady act, Lester? Like my mother? News flash: It ain't happening. You knew that when you married me. You knew that when you decided to take over my daddy's church, and you know that now. And you just seem to forget all that I *have* been doing. I've turned the youth department around. I go to all the little church functions, the boring meetings, the sick and shut-in visits, the stupid bingo games. I even taught some Sunday school classes, and you want to talk to me about being proper?" Rachel was fuming now, too. Granted, maybe she shouldn't have been at the club, but if he'd been doing the right thing—keeping the floozies out of his face—she would've never gone in the first place. "Since when did you get so self-righteous anyway?"

Lester let out an exasperated sigh as he picked up his glass from the table and took it to the sink. "Rachel, I'm just trying to live a godly life and I want my family to do the same." He poured his juice out, then put the glass in the dishwasher before turning back to face her. "You're always talking about your mother, but you could learn a thing or two from her ability to handle things properly. I was talking to your father about this very thing—"

"Why are you talking to my father?" Rachel interrupted.

"Because I don't know how to get you to see that we've got to do better."

"I don't *have* to do anything! You married the wrong person if you want someone like my mother. And if my daddy couldn't change me all those years he tried, I don't know what makes you think you can." Rachel leaned back and crossed her arms. "And for your information, I'm trying to be a proper first lady, as you call it, but I'm not gon' be no fool either. And if you can't do what I ask, then I can't do what you ask."

Lester sighed again. "Fine, Rachel, what do you ask?"

"Keep the skanks out of your face."

Lester nodded. "I will keep the skanks out of my face."

"I'm serious, Lester. 'Cause I can't promise you I won't act a fool."

Lester forced a smile. "You? Act a fool? Never."

"I'm serious, Lester. You know what I'm capable of. Don't make me go there."

"Whatever you say, Rachel. I don't want to argue with you." Lester popped the last piece of toast in his mouth. "I have to get over to the church. The electrician is coming." Lester leaned down and kissed her on the top of the head, which meant he was still salty with her.

Rachel watched him leave. He reminded her so much of her father, from his walk to the way he handled situations. Even his demeanor was like Simon Jackson.

She'd always heard that most women marry a man just like their fathers. She'd just never believed that saying would apply to her.

chapter 12

Angela slid the check to the tall, burly mover and shook his hand. He glanced at the check, which included a hefty tip, and smiled.

"Thank you so much, ma'am. And if you ever need Three Brothers' Movers again, please don't hesitate to call." He smiled again before taking off to the truck.

Angela closed the door, then turned and surveyed her new home. At twenty-five hundred square feet, it was just right for her and Chase. She loved the hardwood floors, spacious kitchen, and oversize living room. She sighed as she looked at all the boxes. What she wouldn't give to go back to Atlanta. She had been looking forward to coming home. Her parents were still here and it would do Chase good to be around his grandparents and cousins. But that quickly diminished after she'd found out how far Jonathan would go to be a part of her son's life.

"Mama! Did you see my room? It's so big!" Chase came barreling down the stairs. He could barely contain his excitement.

"Of course I saw it, baby. I picked it out."

"Man, it is so cool," Chase squealed. "I wish Donnie and Steve could see it." Angela expected Chase to get a little nostalgic when he talked about his best friends back in Atlanta. But he appeared to have forgotten them already, especially when he noticed the group of boys riding their bikes outside. "Can I go play outside? I wanna meet them boys riding their bikes."

"Yes, you may go outside and introduce yourself to *those* boys riding their bikes," Angela said.

Chase ignored her correction and ran outside. Angela smiled. He had never been a shy child. He was such a handsome little boy. He had a head full of curly hair and beautiful brown eyes. Unfortunately, he was the spitting image of his father. It had taken months of counseling for Angela to get over the nauseous feeling she would get every time she looked at him. She would find herself staring at Chase and playing out every moment of her relationship with Jonathan, trying to figure out signs she missed, how she couldn't have known her husband was gay. And although she hated to admit it, there were times when she'd look at her son, see Jonathan, and find herself getting angry. When she caught Chase playing with Constance's daughter's Barbie doll one day, she'd nearly lost it, screaming and throwing the Barbie doll against the wall. It had scared poor Chase to death. That's when she knew she had to get help.

Angela had been doing well. Counseling had worked and she had tried her best to move on. It had helped that he hadn't really tried to see her. He'd sent money and letters, but she'd never responded. Now, everything was changing.

"And why, pray tell, are you standing here in the middle of your living room with the front door wide open?"

Angela smiled at her mother, whom she hadn't even notice walk up. "Hi, Mom." She reached out and hugged the older woman. "Chase took off to go play and left the door open. I was just staring at him and got lost in thought."

"Umm-hmmm," Mrs. Brooks said as she closed the door. "I saw that little mongrel out there, acting like he didn't want to kiss me around his new friends." She laughed. "I absolutely love this place."

Angela followed her into the kitchen. "That's one of the perks of working in corporate America."

"All these perks just for buying clothes," her mother said, shaking her head.

Angela laughed. There was so much more to her job as a buyer for Macy's. People thought all she did all day was buy clothes. She fumbled in a box and pulled out a large coffeemaker. "Sit down, I'll make us some coffee," she said as she plugged it in.

Mrs. Brooks moved another box and sat down at the kitchen table. "You have your work cut out for you."

"I know. I don't know what I was thinking. I should've had the movers unpack, too."

After fixing both of them a cup of coffee, Angela placed the sugar bowl and cream on the table, then sat down across from her mother.

"So, have you heard from that lowlife, Jonathan Jackson?" Mrs. Brooks snarled.

Angela smiled. You'd think her mother was the one Jonathan had hurt. She hated him with every bone in her body. "No, he hasn't been in contact with me since I got the custody papers, but I'm sure it's just a matter of time."

Mrs. Brooks dropped two sugar cubes in her coffee. "So this silly custody suit is real?"

"Yes, it's very real."

"I tell you what, you better not let my grandson around that fa—"

"Mama!"

Mrs. Brooks shrugged. "What? I call it like I see it. And ain't no sense in sugarcoating it."

"I know, but still."

"Fine, I don't want my grandson around his kind."

"Even if it's his father?"

"Especially if it's his father." Mrs. Brooks sipped her coffee. "I mean, how is that child supposed to understand that?" She shook her head. "And I'm just so disappointed in Reverend Jackson. I hated leaving Zion Hill, but he accepted his son's amoral behavior and that is just wrong."

"I guess you never know how you will react until you're

faced with that situation," Angela responded. She couldn't understand why she was taking up for Jonathan. She definitely didn't agree with his lifestyle choice and she sure as heck didn't forgive him for what he'd done to her. But her mother was so negative about most things, sometimes she made Angela want to look for the positive. Angela shook that thought away. There were no positives in letting Jonathan see Chase.

"Please," Mrs. Brooks responded. "Let your brother come home talking about how he's gay. As much as me and your father love him, he's history. The Bible says that God intended for man to be with woman, not man with man. Such is the righteous path of God."

"You're preaching to the choir, Mama." Angela rubbed her temples. Was this what she was going to have to deal with on a regular basis now?

"Well, you know we will spare no expenses. We'll hire the best lawyers, private investigators, whatever it takes, to win this case." Mrs. Brooks patted Angela's hand. She looked around before leaning in toward her daughter. "Your daddy swore me to secrecy on this because he didn't want you to know." She paused and took a deep breath. "But we already have a private detective following Jonathan."

Angela raised her eyebrows in shock. "What? For what?"

Mrs. Brooks sat back proudly. "You know them funny people engage in deviant sexual behavior. And when Jonathan Jackson goes into one of those gay strip clubs, or picks up some strange man in an adult bookstore, our cameras will be right there to capture him. Once a judge sees those pictures, this will be a nonissue." She smiled like she had it all figured out.

Angela sighed. She definitely didn't agree with her mother's underhanded ways but she knew it was useless to argue. Besides, she did want to do everything possible to keep Jonathan away from Chase. Maybe that meant she would have to play dirty. And after all the pain Jonathan had caused her, she wasn't above getting down and dirty. Was she?

chapter 13

Rachel scanned the shelf, trying to find something to pique her interest. She was looking for a good spiritually based book to help her be strong in dealing with the people of Zion Hill.

She pulled out a new book by Juanita Bynum and started reading the back cover.

"That's a good one. I think I've read it twice."

Rachel turned toward the soft voice. "Hello. Linda Morgan, right?" She remembered the brown-skinned woman with the warm smile from a church leadership conference they had attended together.

Linda nodded. "How are you today, Sister Adams?"

"Fine. How are things at St. Luke's?"

"Same story, different day. But God is keeping me strong."

Rachel couldn't help but smile. Linda was actually one of the nicest first ladies she'd ever met. She'd even sent Rachel a note telling her to call if she ever needed help with anything, although Rachel had never done so.

"Just shopping, or looking for something in particular?" she asked.

"Just looking around, actually." Rachel took in Linda's whole demeanor. She was one of the most respected first ladies in town. Yet she didn't look like a typical first lady. Like now: She had her curly hair pulled back in a ponytail and wore a designer sweat suit. Still, she exuded elegance.

From what Rachel had heard, Linda didn't take any mess from the women at her church—even though Pastor Morgan was one of the most handsome preachers in town. As Rachel studied her, she doubted that this woman ever had to get ignorant like she had with Nikki Rollins last week. Rachel suddenly felt the need to open up to her.

"Sister Morgan, when you get some free time, can I talk to you?"

"I'm free right now." Linda set down the stationery she had been holding. "I'll just get this another time."

Rachel put her book back on the shelf. "Can I buy you a cup of coffee?"

"Sure."

They walked across the street to Starbucks, where both of them ordered a venti café mocha, then took a seat on the coffee shop's patio.

"How do you stay strong? I mean, with people at the church and their expectations," Rachel asked after they had made small talk for a few minutes.

"Prayer, honey, lots and lots of prayer."

"But I bet the women at St. Luke's don't try you like they try me. I mean, if they're not trying to come on to my husband, they're disrespecting me or gossiping about me." Rachel couldn't believe she was being so candid, but she'd finally found someone she felt could relate to her plight.

Linda smiled. "You forget, I've been first lady for thirteen years. Believe me when I tell you, they tried me. I just had to let them know they couldn't get away with it."

"That's what I'm trying to do, but everyone's giving me a hard time about it." Rachel sighed heavily.

Linda slowly sipped her coffee. "Maybe it's the way you're going about it," she finally said.

"What do you mean?"

"How do you put these women in their places?"

"I go off on them," Rachel replied, like that was the only possible answer.

"That's what they expect you to do. And that only gives them ammunition," Linda said. "You have to take the high road."

Rachel sucked her teeth and shook her head. "Unh-unh. My mom took the high road. I can't do that." As much as she loved her mother, Rachel had vowed to never be like her—submissive and soft-spoken. Granted, her mother had put people in their place when push came to shove, but Rachel didn't have that kind of patience. She had to let these people know she wasn't playing from the get-go.

"Oh, I knew Loretta, bless her heart. She was the epitome

of a strong, black woman. But she was a rare breed. That's not me." Linda flashed a smile.

"Me either." Rachel was glad someone could understand where she was coming from.

"You know what," Linda said. "Why don't you come to the First Ladies Council—it's an organization of first ladies here in Houston. We meet monthly to exchange ideas and offer support."

Rachel had heard about the group, but she'd figured they were a bunch of stuffy old women who would stand in judgment of her.

"I don't know."

As if she were reading Rachel's mind, Linda said, "Don't worry about putting on airs. We all try to be ourselves when we get together. Most of our days are spent trying to fit into a particular mold, so when we're together we're footloose and fancy-free." She grinned. "Please, come as my guest. We meet at St. Luke's this Saturday. Just one meeting. If you like it, come back. If you don't, no harm done."

Rachel considered the idea. "Sure, why not?"

Linda stood. "Then it's a date. We'll see you Saturday."

Rachel stood as well and leaned in and hugged Linda. "Thank you very much."

"You're welcome. Until then, stay prayerful," Linda said.

"I'll do that," Rachel replied.

A whole group of women who understood what she was going through? Come to think of it, Rachel thought, that's exactly what she needed.

chapter 14

Jonathan ducked down in his seat as the football came tumbling toward his car. The lanky boy with two missing front teeth didn't look his way as he retrieved the ball and tossed it back to his friends. Jonathan eased up and smiled as he watched Chase throw the ball. He'd been sitting outside Angela's house, watching his son for the last hour. It had taken days of detective work, but he'd finally found out where she lived by renting a car and following her mother over here two days ago.

It had torn at his heart not to be able to go and talk to his son. What was especially sad was that Chase probably wouldn't know who he was even if he did go and talk to him. Jonathan wondered what Angela had told Chase about him.

He hoped she hadn't made him out to be some sick, confused individual.

Chase seemed so happy playing with his new friends. He was an adorable little boy and Jonathan could see himself in every inch of the little boy's face. This was the closest Jonathan had ever been to him. Angela had moved before she gave birth and he didn't find out where she lived until Chase was nearly two years old. He had had to go through the church files to locate a forwarding address for her tithing statement. Then he'd flown to Atlanta and had done exactly what he was doing now, sitting outside their house and watching his son. Angela and Chase looked so content; Jonathan couldn't help but wish they had all stayed a happy little family. What would his life have been like if he had stayed married to Angela and kept his secret forever?

Jonathan was so lost in thought that the vibrating phone in his jacket pocket caused him to jump. He fumbled trying to get it out of his pocket.

"Hello," he answered.

"Hey, big brother. What's going on?" Rachel's voice bellowed through the phone.

"Hey, little sister. Nothing much."

"Nothing? Did you see Chase?"

Jonathan sighed. It had been Rachel's idea that he try to see his son. Only Rachel had suggested that he walk right up to the door and ring the bell and demand that Angela let him see Chase.

"Yeah, I saw him," Jonathan said.

"Oh, wow," Rachel responded. "How does he look? Did he

know who you are? When are we going to meet him? I bet Nia is going to love him."

"Whoa, slow down, Rachel. I didn't talk to him."

"Why? Angela wouldn't let you?" Rachel's tone immediately changed.

"No, I didn't even go in," he admitted.

"Why not, Jonathan? We talked about this. You have just as much right to that child as she does."

"I don't know, I'm just trying to take things slow." Jonathan rubbed his bald head. This whole situation was stressing him out.

"You need to give him a chance to meet you before you go to court. That way he won't act all scared."

Jonathan was just about to respond when something hit the driver's-side window. He jumped and almost dropped the phone.

"What do you think you're doing?" Angela shouted, banging on the window.

Jonathan got his bearings then spoke into the phone. "Rachel, I need to call you back." He snapped his cell phone closed before she could say anything. He opened the door and stepped out of the car.

"Hi, Angela," he said, facing her.

"Don't hi me. I wanna know what you're doing outside my house!"

"I was just in the neighborhood and well . . ."

"Stop lying! Are you spying on us? How did you find out where we lived?"

Jonathan sighed. "Angela, I'm trying to be there for my son. You won't let me near him, so I have to see him however I can."

Angela looked like she was fighting back tears. Jonathan felt horrible for her. She was still as beautiful as ever. He was a little shocked at the closely cropped hairdo she now wore, especially because it was dyed a light golden brown. Although it looked good on her, it was so out of character for the Angela he knew. The thing that got him the most, though, was her beautiful almond-shaped eyes. They now bore the look of a woman who had seen her share of pain. It hurt his heart to know that he'd caused that pain.

"I can't believe you," Angela continued. "Why are you doing this to us? Why won't you just leave us alone?"

"I can't do that," Jonathan softly said. "It's killed me not being a part of my son's life." He suddenly smiled as Chase came racing over. He wanted to take him in his arms and shower him with kisses.

"Hey, Mommy. My new friends say I'm way cool," Chase beamed. He turned toward Jonathan. "Hello, my name is Chase. I just moved here." Chase held out his hand, which Jonathan shook gently. Chase had a huge grin across his face. "Are you my mommy's new friend? I have five new friends already."

"Hi, Chase. My name is Jonathan and I'm an old friend of your mommy's."

Chase cocked his head and squinted his eyes. "Mr. Jonathan, you look like that picture my mommy has hidden in her dresser drawer."

Angela looked like she wanted to clamp her hand over his mouth and shut him up.

"My mommy said that's a picture of my daddy," Chase continued.

Jonathan felt his heart drop. So Angela had told Chase about him.

"My daddy was the best," Chase boasted proudly. His expression suddenly turned solemn. "He died when I was just a baby."

Angela had heard enough. She put her hands on Chase's shoulders and turned him toward her. "Sweetie, let's not bore this man with our stories. Why don't you go back and play with your friends, or better yet, go ask them if they want to come in and get some Kool Kups."

Chase's eyes lit up at the prospect of the frozen Kool-Aid cups. "Wow!" He took off to where his friends were still playing without even saying good-bye.

Angela watched him run off.

"You told him I was dead?" Jonathan asked. He never imagined Angela would stoop that low.

"You're dead to us," she replied coolly.

He tried to fight back the anger that was building in the pit of his stomach. "Well, you're just going to have to tell him you lied."

Angela folded her arms. "I don't have to tell *my* son anything I don't want to tell him." She stepped in close. "You listen to me, Jonathan Edward Jackson. You chose your life; you have no say-so in ours. Stay the hell away from my house, my child, and me!"

Jonathan looked at Angela in shock. This was so not the woman he knew standing before him right now. This woman was filled not just with pain, but with hate.

"I won't be denied my child any longer," he said, matter-of-factly.

Angela looked like she wanted to kill him right there in the middle of the street. "I swear to God, you don't know who you're messing with. But you will."

With that she turned and stormed up the steps to her house.

chapter 15

Rachel entered the conference room at St. Luke's and stared at the group of women seated at the mahogany table. She suddenly felt uneasy. These women were seasoned first ladies. Take Dorothy Rattlin, who was seated at the head of the table, looking like a CEO of a major company. She'd been a first lady for one of Houston's mega churches for a gazillion years. And Donna Childs? Shoot! Her husband served on the board of the University of Houston. Not to mention Suzanne Caldron, whose husband had been a spiritual advisor to Clinton when he was in office. These were some major players. What in the world was she doing here?

She was about to bolt when Linda spotted her. "Rachel, I'm so glad you could make it." She walked over and hugged Rachel, before taking her hand and leading her to the table.

The women stopped talking and looked at Rachel, who suddenly felt self-conscious in her Baby Phat blouse and capri pants.

"Ladies, this is Rachel Adams; her husband is pastor of Zion Hill," Linda said.

The women smiled warmly at her, easing her nervousness.

"Please, have a seat," Dorothy said.

"And welcome," Suzanne added.

Rachel sat down and quickly scanned the room. In all, there were about twenty women there. Linda sat in the seat next to her.

"We were just finishing up some business about a citywide charity event we're hosting," Dorothy said.

Rachel smiled as they continued their business. She was actually intrigued with all that they were doing, because many of their ideas were along the same lines as hers.

Thirty minutes later, they were wrapping up the business part of their meeting. "Well, I think we've had a productive meeting," Dorothy said. "Now, to my favorite part: What's bothering you this week?"

Several of the women chuckled.

Rachel's eyes lit up. Did they actually come here and discuss all their personal business? Were they actually truthful about the stuff that was bugging them?

Linda leaned in and whispered, "Don't worry, we have sort of a code that what's talked about here, stays here. You will be amazed at how refreshing it feels to be able to release some of your frustrations."

Rachel gave her a look of approval. She was loving the council already.

"Let me go first," said a woman Rachel didn't recognize. "For those of you who don't know me, I'm Sharony Livingston, first lady of New Bethel. I just want to say that I'm sick and tired of my church members who have no regard for the pastor's family. They want him at events that are not even related to church! George had to leave dinner last week because one of the members was buying her daughter her first car and she wanted her pastor there because it was a special occasion." Sharony dramatically rolled her eyes.

Several women in the room nodded like they could definitely relate.

"You ain't never lied," another lady added. "Louis hasn't been home one night out of the whole month because everybody's got somewhere they want him to be. They could care less about the fact that he has two kids of his own that he never sees."

Rachel felt like she was in the Twilight Zone. Where had this group been all her life?

"Speaking of kids, if one more person tries to pump my children for information about what's going on between me and my husband, I'm going to lose it," another woman added.

"Oooh, I hate that," Suzanne said. "But you have to learn to be quiet and pray about it and let God handle it."

"Well, I definitely need you all to say an extra prayer for me, because if one more woman bats her eyes at my husband or wiggles her big butt trying to get his attention, I think I'm going to lose it," a woman sitting toward the end of the table said.

"Gloria, I don't know why you keep letting those women get to you. You know they're just trying you," Donna said.

Rachel definitely could understand that. She felt like she was being tried on a regular basis.

"I know some of them are trying me," Gloria replied. "For some, it's not even about me. They just want my husband to notice them. But I have to be honest, I'm scared that one day he's just going to give in to the temptation."

"Ladies," Dorothy said, trying to regain control of the meeting. "Remember, we want these to be more than just gripe sessions." She turned to Sharony. "Sister Livingston, you have got to put your foot down with the congregation and your husband. Let him know you and your children need him just as much as the members do."

Rachel fought back a smile. Her mother could've definitely benefited from this group because Lord knew, she'd rarely put her foot down when it came to Simon. Rachel was especially impressed with the candid way the women spoke.

"And Gloria," Dorothy continued, "as we tell you every meeting, you've got to turn that over to God, or you're going to drive yourself crazy. You've got to trust your husband, pray that he continues to be strong, and know that if and when something ever does happen, it will be revealed to you. Until then, there's no need to drive yourself crazy with worry. Too often, we as women try to fix things."

"When what we need to do is go to the ultimate handyman, Jesus," Donna added.

Gloria nodded like she knew they were right, but Rachel could tell from the look on her face she was having a hard time with it.

Linda patted Gloria's hand and said, "You have to keep in mind that the members' expectations of their pastor and his family are often based on *their* opinions of what he should be and not on the Bible."

"Like hats," Donna chimed in. "I hate hats, but some member is always trying to get me to wear one because 'that's what first ladies are supposed to do.' "

Dorothy nodded. "You have to be strong and just make sure you don't lose yourself in other people's image of who you're supposed to be." She looked at Rachel. "But let's see if our guest would like to jump in. Sister Adams, anything you'd like to get off your chest?"

Boy, there weren't enough hours in the day for Rachel to say what was on her mind. But she figured she'd start with the thing that was bugging her the most. "I can't get the members at my church to respect me. I try to be who they want me to be—to an extent anyway. I try to be friendly with the members—most of them, at least. I work hard for the church, but they still don't respect me. I mean, maybe it's because I'm only twenty-seven, I don't know."

"Maybe it's because you wear low-cut Baby Phat blouses and tight blue jean capris," one of the women mumbled.

Rachel's eyes grew wide. Dorothy threw an admonishing

look at the woman, who shrugged and said, "I just said what you all were thinking."

Dorothy smiled at Rachel. "As you can see, we believe in being honest here. And while Sister Murray could've found a more tactful way to put it, she's right."

Rachel looked down at her top. She hadn't thought anything about it when she threw it on this morning, except that it was cute.

"Sweetie," Linda interjected, "no one wants you to change who you are, but there's a time and a place for everything. Unfortunately, you have to earn respect, and wearing hip-hop clothes, going off on people, and going to clubs is not the way to do it."

"How'd you know about the club?"

Suzanne laughed. "Girl, you know how your people are. We heard about the club probably before you even left the club."

Rachel was so embarrassed, but she said gently, "I don't understand what the big deal is about having a little fun. I didn't get drunk, or dance provocatively, or anything like that."

"I hate to tell you, Rachel, but there *is* something wrong with that. It's like you said, you're young, not only in age, but in your walk with God," Donna added. "Ask yourself, as a role model in the church, do you think you hanging out at the club is pleasing in God's eyes?"

Rachel didn't respond. She was definitely starting to feel bad, but Donna reached over and gently touched her hand. "But don't feel bad. Just learn from it, grow from it. We've all done and said things over the years we wish we could take back."

"Ain't that the truth," several people muttered as laughter rippled through the room.

"While no one suggests that you lose yourself, you do need to elevate yourself. Sometimes that may mean walking away from a confrontation," Linda continued. Her voice was so gentle that Rachel didn't take offense.

"Sometimes it may mean leaving the Baby Phat and the Apple Bottoms on the rack in the store," Sister Murray added.

Several people shook their heads at her.

"What? She walked up in here looking like JLo." Sister Murray shot a look like she meant every word she was saying.

"I hope you don't get offended by anything we tell you, but we're all here to help each other grow," Dorothy said, cutting her eyes at Sister Murray again.

Rachel looked down, surprised that she wasn't upset. Actually, she was starting to wonder if Sister Murray had a point. Rachel didn't want to lose herself, but at the same time, she did want to change some things about herself.

"No, ladies, I really appreciate your honesty," she said. They'd given her a lot to think about.

"So does that mean you'll be back?" Donna asked.

"Most definitely." Rachel finally smiled.

"Amen. That's what I like to hear. Well, until next time, sisters," Dorothy said. "Meeting is adjourned."

chapter 16

Jonathan drove up to his father's house. He really was in no mood to deal with anyone. He hadn't been right since his confrontation with Angela two days ago. He wished David could've taken their father to his doctor's appointment, but—of course—David "had something else to do," so as usual, the burden fell on him. Normally, he didn't mind. Today, though, he was just in a foul mood.

Jonathan slowed down, then pulled into the driveway. David was standing in front of the house arguing with a scraggly looking woman. She kept trying to put her arms around him and he kept pushing her away.

Jonathan stepped out of his car. As he got closer, he realized that the woman was David's ex-girlfriend, Tawny. She looked like she was at least eight months' pregnant.

"What's up, Tawny?" Jonathan said as he walked up to them. She didn't speak and instead lowered her eyes and started rubbing her arms nervously. It was obvious that she was high. "Tawny, what are you doing? Are you still doin' drugs while you're pregnant?"

David pursed his lips. Jonathan could tell his brother was furious. "Jon, man. Go on in the house. I got this."

Jonathan wanted to say more, but the sight of Tawny standing there in a tattered flowered dress, which—despite her pregnancy—swallowed her body, black leggings, and house shoes was absolutely heartbreaking.

He shook his head as he walked in the house. He noticed the open living room window, and although he knew he shouldn't eavesdrop on his brother, Jonathan tossed his car keys on the table and eased onto the sofa so he could hear the conversation outside.

"Tawny, I can't believe you're doing this," David said.

"Oh, quit trippin'," Tawny whined. "Just gimme some money."

"I am not giving you any money. You disappear for four months. I didn't know if you were dead or alive."

"Well, you the one broke up with me."

"Because you won't leave the drugs alone. I told you I'm not with that anymore." David sighed and pointed at her stomach. "And when you come back, you come back pregnant? And still getting high?"

Tawny let out an exasperated sigh. "Please don't start with that mess. Just 'cause you done went and got all holy on me, don't make you Jesus' personal assistant or nothing."

It was David's turn to sigh. "Have you even been to the doctor?"

"Why you asking all these questions? I guess you wanna know is it your baby, too."

"Is it?"

"Awww, no you didn't!"

Jonathan couldn't see Tawny but he knew she was wiggling her neck, about to go off. Tawny was a wild child if he'd ever seen one; the best thing David had ever done was let her go.

"Tawny, I can't do this with you." He sounded like he was completely stressed out.

"Well, just gimme some money and then call me Casper." She laughed at her own corny joke.

David hesitated. "Tell you what. Meet me at the Houston Women's Clinic tomorrow at eleven. After we do a checkup, I'll give you some money."

Jonathan hoped his brother was lying because any money he gave Tawny was going straight to Big Don, the neighborhood drug dealer. The sad part was that, from what his brother had told him, Tawny used to be a beautiful woman who was headed places. Until she hooked up with a drug dealer who got her strung out.

At their mother's deathbed, David had promised Loretta he would get clean. As far as Jonathan knew, he'd kept that promise. David had tried to stay with Tawny, but it had just proven to be too difficult.

"Come on, David. Gimme some money," Tawny pleaded.

"Tomorrow, Tawny. That's it."

"How much you gon' give me?"

"Just be there at eleven o'clock and you'll see." With that, David came into the house. He didn't even notice Jonathan as he stormed upstairs to his room.

Jonathan didn't think as he jumped up and raced outside to follow Tawny, who was headed up the sidewalk, bobbing her head to some imaginary music.

"Tawny, wait up," Jonathan called.

Tawny spun around and flashed a cheesy grin. "What's crack-a-lackin', brotha-in-law?" She seemed in a much better mood now that she knew she was getting some money.

Jonathan wanted to tell her she was the only thing "crackin'" around here. Instead, he said, "I just wanted to see how you're doing."

"I'm as straight as fish grease."

He had no idea what that meant but nodded anyway.

"Let me hold forty dollars," she quickly said. "I'm about to hit a lick and I'll pay you back."

"I'm broke, Tawny," he said, patting his pockets.

She walked closer to him. "Awww, come on. I'll hook you up real good." She rubbed her hands up and down her body as she wiggled her hips. "I know your brother done told you about all this here. Don't fight it. You know you want it. Fifty dollars."

Jonathan tried to keep down the bile rising in his throat. "Ummm, I think I'll pass."

Tawny frowned. "Oh, yeah. That's right, you funny. Well, look here, you can do me in the butt. Seventy-five dollars. You can even call me Frank or something. I don't care."

Jonathan shook his head, trying not to go off on her silly behind. "Tawny, I just wanted to check on you. With you expecting and all, I just wanted to make sure you were all right."

She smiled again as she rubbed her stomach. "Yeah, David's gon' be a daddy."

Jonathan knew he needed to tread lightly, but he had to ask. "Are you sure? I mean . . . I thought you and David broke up a while ago."

She spread her legs and slapped her hands on her hips. "And? David came tiptoeing back around me. I know it's his because I wasn't with anybody else the week I got pregnant. So there."

Jonathan nodded. "Well, are you taking care of yourself?"

"Who are you? Dr. Spock? Dang, you and your brother 'bout to work my nerves." She turned and started walking off. "You gon' make me miss my bus. Tell David I'll see him tomorrow. Tell him I ain't playing with him neither. He betta have some money."

Jonathan shook his head as she walked off. He couldn't help but think how students should be required to spend a day with people like Tawny. That would be a sure way to prevent drug abuse.

chapter 17

Jonathan fiddled with a magazine as he waited for his father outside the doctor's office.

"So, how'd it go?" he asked as Simon walked out.

"As well as can be expected." Simon kept walking. Jonathan knew his father wouldn't say much else. He'd revealed the fact that he had prostate cancer, promised to get treatment, and then refused to talk about it anymore. The only thing he would say was that if it was his time to go, it was just his time to go.

"So, have you made any contact with Angela?" Simon asked once they were in the car and heading home.

Jonathan sighed. "Naw, she just doesn't want to have anything to do with me." He paused. "Can I ask you something? Do you think I'm wrong for wanting to see my son?"

Simon shifted uncomfortably in the passenger seat. "Jonathan, you know I have issues with your lifestyle. Always have. Always will."

Jonathan nodded.

"But," Simon continued, "that is your child. And I can't condone Angela keeping you from him. I understand the girl being hurt. But it's been seven years. Time to let past hurts heal."

"I couldn't agree with you more, Dad." Jonathan pulled onto the freeway. "Let's just hope a judge agrees with you as well."

They rode in silence the rest of the way home.

"You coming in?" Simon asked as they pulled up in front of his house.

Jonathan debated whether he should go inside. But then he realized that he had nothing to rush home for. "Sure, why not?"

They made their way inside and found David at Simon's desk, vigorously punching in numbers on a calculator.

"Boy, what are you doing?" Simon asked.

David looked up, like they'd broken his deep concentration. "Oh, I'm just trying to figure some stuff out."

Simon walked over to the desk. "Figure what out?" He looked down at the paper David had been writing on. "What's this?"

"Nothing." David tried to snatch it back, but Simon moved it out of the way.

"Rent. Utilities," he read. "You finally moving?" David didn't respond as Simon turned his attention back to the paper. "Day care? What in the world?"

David stood up and with a firm voice announced, "I'm getting my child."

"Excuse me?" Jonathan said.

"I said, I'm getting my son. I'm going to raise him."

Simon looked at David like he was crazy. "And how, pray tell, are you going to do that?"

"It ain't like I'll be the first single father in the country." He threw his pen down defiantly. "You ain't gotta believe I can do this. Ain't nobody gotta believe it. As long as I believe it, I can do it."

"What are you, a Nike commercial now?" Jonathan said.

"Man, it ain't like I got much choice," David replied.

Jonathan shook his head in disbelief. "Shouldn't you even wait and make sure the baby is yours?"

"It is mine. I know exactly when it happened."

Jonathan shrugged. "Well, I'm just saying. How are you going to take care of a child?"

"The best way I know how. I don't have a choice, Jon. Tawny can't do it. I have to man up."

David glanced at his father like he was expecting him to say something smart.

Instead, Simon stood there with a smile on his face. "Son, I don't think I've ever been more proud of you."

Jonathan thought about what David was saying. Why was he giving him a hard time about doing the right thing? He finally smiled at his brother as well. No matter how far-fetched the idea was, David's heart was in the right place, and Jonathan couldn't help it—he had never been more proud of his brother either.

chapter 18

Rachel moved the chair back into place. She had just finished preparing for a meeting with her youth group, The Good Girlz. She'd started the group six months ago to work with wayward teen girls and help them walk the right path. They did a lot of community service activities, like volunteering at the senior citizens' center and mentoring younger girls. In addition, she'd found helping the girls in the small group to be very therapeutic for herself since she'd had such a drama-filled teenage life.

Tonight, the girls were watching a film on building self-esteem. Some sorority girls from the AKA chapter at Texas Southern University were also coming by to make a presentation on the topic. Everyone, Rachel included, was pretty excited about it.

Rachel had gotten everything together and still had a good three hours or so before tonight's meeting. "Just enough time to run home and take a quick nap," she mumbled to herself as she turned off the light in the conference room.

Rachel called Twyla as soon as she got in the car to remind her that she'd agreed to come to church Sunday. Since she didn't have any real friends at church, Rachel had been trying to get Twyla more involved at Zion Hill. Twyla had joined about six months ago, but she hadn't done much except come to service, and even that was sporadic.

She'd just hung up after leaving Twyla a message when her cell phone rang. She looked at the number and couldn't place it. She debated answering, then decided to go ahead. "Hello, this is Rachel."

"Mrs. Adams?"

"Yes, this is she."

"This is Mrs. Ward, the principal at Jordan's school. Can you come up to the school right away? Jordan has been suspended for fighting."

"Fighting!" Rachel wanted to scream. That boy was going to drive her insane.

"Yes, and Mrs. Adams, this may be the last straw. We can't continue to have these discipline and academic problems with Jordan." The woman sounded completely exasperated.

"I'm on my way." Rachel pressed the End button on her phone. This was her fifth call from Jordan's school in the last three weeks. Once for fighting. Another for getting smart with his teacher. Twice for not doing his homework. Rachel was at her wits' end. She immediately dialed Lester's number and felt her blood boil when it went straight to his voice mail. She hadn't heard from him all day. She knew he was at some church conference in Galveston, but at least he could answer his phone at some point. She left a short message.

"This is just a repeat of my daddy!" Rachel snapped as she threw the phone down onto the passenger seat. Growing up, one of the things she'd hated most about her father was the fact that he was always off on some church business. Now here was her husband doing the same thing.

Rachel's phone rang and she snatched it up, hoping it was her husband. "Lester?" she said, not bothering with the caller ID.

"Umm, no. It's Bobby."

Rachel rubbed her temples. "What's going on, Bobby?" She wasn't in the mood to deal with him right now.

"You tell me. Jordan called me and said he's been suspended."

"He called you?"

"He asked me to come get him."

She let out a long sigh.

"Rachel, what is going on? I mean, he seemed fine last time I had him. This is getting ridiculous," Bobby said.

Rachel had been trying her best to hold it in, but she couldn't help it; she felt the tears begin to form. "Bobby, I don't know what's wrong with that boy. He is driving me crazy!"

"I know you said you'd been having problems, but I didn't know it was this bad."

"Well, it is."

"Look, are you on your way to the school?"

"Yes."

"I'll meet you there."

Rachel wiped her eyes in relief. "Okay."

Twenty minutes later, both Rachel and Bobby were sitting in Mrs. Ward's office. A bruised-up Jordan was sitting in the corner, a scowl on his face.

"I'm sure you can understand our position. This is Jordan's third major infraction, in addition to all the minor ones. We simply cannot allow him to remain at the Rice Academy."

Rachel glared at Jordan. They had paid all this money for him to go to this exclusive private school and he was over here acting a fool.

"It is our suggestion that he be placed in an alternative learning center until he gets his behavior under control," Mrs. Ward said.

Bobby looked stunned.

"Mrs. Ward, on behalf of my son, let me apologize," Rachel said. "I want to thank you for your trouble." She stood and shook Mrs. Ward's hand. The matronly principal gave her a sympathetic look before returning her handshake.

They had barely made it to the parking lot before Rachel spun on Jordan. "Boy, what is your problem?"

Jordan just shrugged.

"I ought to beat the living daylights out of you!"

Bobby caught her arm and pulled her back.

"Rachel, chill. You're in the middle of the parking lot at his school," Bobby said.

"I don't care! As God is my witness, I'm gon' hurt this child." Rachel's chest was heaving. It was a good thing Bobby grabbed her because if she had struck Jordan once, she probably wouldn't have stopped.

"Look here, I have an idea. Why don't we let Jordan stay with me a couple of days while we try to figure this out? Maybe I can talk to him and see what the problem is," Bobby suggested. Jordan's eyes seemed to light up at that idea.

Rachel really didn't know if that was the answer, but she knew right about now, she didn't even want to be around Jordan; there was no telling what she might do. She knew Lester wouldn't approve of Jordan going to his father's, but they had tried everything else under the sun. Maybe Bobby could succeed where they had failed.

"You know what, take him. Maybe you can get through to him, because I dang sure can't." Rachel got in her car and sped off without even saying good-bye to her son. As soon as she did, though, her anger subsided and sadness crept up on her as she reflected on her relationship with Jordan. She didn't want to be mean, but she was at her wits' end. Maybe this tough-love route was the way to go. She didn't know, but at this point she'd try anything to get her son back on the right track.

Desperately, she called Lester again. Once again she got his voice mail. Why was it that her husband was AWOL in her hour of need, yet her ex-lover was right there, willing to help her deal with this crisis?

chapter 19

Lester stared at Rachel, trying to weigh his words carefully. "So explain this to me again," he said. That little vein in his head was pulsing, so she could tell he was getting angry.

"I said, Jordan got suspended from school and he's gone to stay with Bobby for a few days, maybe permanently." They were in Jordan's sports-themed room. Rachel was throwing her son's clothes into a suitcase. Lester stood in the doorway staring at her.

"And you didn't think I needed to be consulted on this?" Lester said.

"I tried to call you several times; you were obviously too busy since all I got was your voice mail. Did you even check your phone?" Rachel snidely remarked as she passed by him and out of the room. She carried Jordan's suitcase downstairs and set it on the kitchen floor. Lester followed her. She could tell he was upset, but she didn't care. He hadn't gotten home from his conference until well after midnight last night and didn't even realize Jordan was gone until this morning.

"So you sent our son to live somewhere else without even talking to me about it?"

Rachel turned to face him. "It's not just somewhere else. It's with his father. And I tried to talk to you about it. But just like my father, you were too busy to tend to your family."

"Here we go with this again," Lester said. "I swear, I'm so sick of this argument. I try to take care of my obligations at the church and make sure I'm keeping you and the kids happy. Ninety percent of the time, when you call, I come running. But one of the few times I'm not available, you run off and do something stupid like this. *We* can handle Jordan's problems."

"Can we, Lester? Because it doesn't look to me like we have."

"Mmph, doesn't surprise *me* that she would do something like this." Both Lester and Rachel turned to Lester's grandmother, Naomi. She was standing in the kitchen doorway holding Nia's hand. "I rang the doorbell, but I guess y'all were too busy arguing to hear, so Nia let me in."

"Nia, what have I told you about opening that front door?" Rachel snapped.

"Please. She saw it was me," Naomi snapped back. She leaned down to Nia. "Sweet Pea, go get your backpack.

109

Grandma is here to pick you up." Nia giggled and ran to her room. Naomi walked into the kitchen, her gaze directed at Lester.

"I tried to tell you, baby. Not only does she not act like a proper first lady, she doesn't act like a proper wife."

Rachel shot the old woman a nasty look. Naomi would never let her live down her past and she'd probably go to her grave thinking Rachel wasn't good enough for Lester.

"Grandma, please let me handle this," Lester said.

"Don't look to me like you know how to handle her at all." Naomi shook her head.

Rachel bit her lip. She and Naomi had gotten along just fine until Lester decided to marry her. Since then, the old woman couldn't stand her. She thought that Rachel was too "worldly" for her precious Lester, whom she had raised.

"Please don't start with me today, Mrs. Naomi," Rachel said. "I told you if you're going to come to my house, you need to stay out of my business."

Naomi glared at Rachel before turning back to her grandson. "It's a doggone shame you let her disrespect your old, fragile grandmother like this. You need to put a leash on your wife. I never, ever would've dreamed of disrespecting your granddaddy's mama. Just shows you what type of women the world is producing today."

Rachel took a deep breath. It was bad enough she had to deal with Naomi in the first place, but she was not about to take this in her own house. "You know what? Lester knew how I was before he married me—"

"Everybody knew how you were. That's why I told him not to marry you," Naomi said, cutting her off.

Rachel spun around toward Lester. "Lester . . ."

Lester sighed heavily. "Rachel, you know how she is when she hasn't had her medication."

Rachel was so sick of Lester and his excuses for his grandmother. Like her being on medication gave her carte blanche to say and do whatever she pleased. "I don't care. I'm not dealing with this."

"Rachel, I think our problems are greater than my grandmother."

"Well, get her out of our business."

Lester turned to his grandmother, who seemed to be enjoying the fight. "Grandma, can you please go check on Nia? I'll come pick you up and take you to dinner later."

"Ooooh, can you take me to Pappadeaux?"

"Yes, Granny."

Naomi squeezed her grandson's cheek, sneered at Rachel, and wobbled out of the room.

Rachel folded her arms and glared at her husband. "Pappadeaux? When's the last time you took *me* to Pappadeaux?"

Lester took a deep breath. "Rachel, why do you insist on making things difficult?"

"Lester, I'm about tired of you!"

"The feeling's mutual, Rachel." Lester shook his head as he grabbed his keys off of the bar.

"What? What is that supposed to mean?" Rachel followed behind him.

Lester spun on Rachel like he'd been waiting to get some stuff off of his chest. "Do you know how many women at that church would die to have your spot? Who would love to say they're first lady and would work every day to uphold all that that entails?"

No, he is not threatening me. Lester used to be meek and shy, but since he'd become pastor of Zion Hill, he'd been getting beside himself. "Let me tell you for the thousandth time, I don't care what anyone else thinks, wants, says—nothing. And no you didn't just threaten me with another woman."

"I wasn't threatening you. I was merely stating a fact," he replied defiantly.

"Oh, now that I done helped you get rid of all the zits, beef up, and get some braces to straighten out your crooked teeth, now you think you're Denzel or somebody and can get whoever you want?"

"I didn't say that."

"Then what are you saying, Lester? Because if you think there's someone out there better than me, then I suggest you go find her."

"Stop being dramatic, Rachel, and let's get back to the issue at hand. How dare you send Jordan out of this house without talking to me? Even though you don't act like it, I am the man of this house."

Rachel stared at her husband trying to flex. Being a big-time minister must have empowered him or something. She couldn't help it. She burst out laughing.

"What in God's name is so funny?"

"You are." Rachel leaned in toward her husband. "Contrary to you and your grandma's belief, you can't put a leash on me, and trying to do so would be a big mistake. If you want some say-so in what goes on with Jordan, then you need to be around when something needs to be said."

Rachel reached over and grabbed her purse before picking up Jordan's suitcase. "I'm going to drop Jordan's stuff off. This conversation is over." Rachel left before Lester could get in another word.

chapter 20

Rachel rubbed her feet as she sat in the driver's seat of her car. She was exhausted after spending the day with Nia and her friends at the Galleria. This morning, she'd taken Nia to a Girl Scout meeting, then driven five of the girls to a birthday party at the ice skating rink. She'd ended up staying and actually had a great time. Nia was now in the backseat, knocked out.

Rachel glanced at her watch. It was still early and she didn't feel like going home and dealing with Lester. He was still mad at her about Jordan and hadn't spoken to her in the two days since. "Let me go check on Daddy," Rachel muttered as she pulled out of the mall parking lot.

It didn't take long for her to arrive at her father's house. She parked and tried to wake Nia up. After realizing Nia had no interest in moving, she smiled and gently picked her daughter up. Rachel let herself in and carried Nia back to her father's bedroom. She laid Nia across the bed and lovingly smiled as she watched her daughter sleep. Nia was her heart. If she hadn't done anything else right in her life, she definitely had done good with her little girl.

Rachel flicked the light out and headed to the den to look for her father. She found him in his usual spot, in front of the TV. He didn't get around much anymore. In fact, he looked like a shell of his usual vibrant self.

"Hey, Daddy," Rachel said as she walked over and kissed her father on the head. He must've been dozing off, because he jumped up, startled.

"Hey, baby girl," Simon said, as he squeezed her hand. "I'm just watching a little *Sanford and Son.*"

"It looks like *Sanford and Son* is watching you," Rachel responded. Their once tumultuous relationship had improved dramatically over the years. Now, Simon was constantly trying to make up for the years of neglect.

"I didn't know if you were asleep so I just let myself in. Nia's in your room asleep. I came to check on you . . ." Her words trailed off as a tall, middle-aged woman walked into the den carrying a tray of food.

"Mrs. Brenda?" Rachel asked in confusion. Why was Deacon Baird's sister, a longtime Zion Hill member, up in her father's home?

"Hi, Rachel." Brenda flashed a smile and walked over to

Simon. She set the tray down next to him, grabbed a napkin, fluffed it out, and placed it on Simon's lap. Then she picked the tray up and placed it on Simon's lap. He smiled at her.

"You need anything else, Reverend?" she said.

Simon gave her a genuine smile, not the fake one Rachel was used to seeing him give the women of the church. "Nothing—at the moment."

Rachel gazed back and forth between the two. She looked closer at Brenda. "Ummm, is that my mother's apron?"

"Oh, I just pulled an apron out of the pantry while I fixed Simon, I mean the reverend, some dinner," Brenda said.

Rachel looked at her father in amazement. "Daddy, she's wearing Mama's apron."

"Baby, calm down. I'm sure Loretta wouldn't mind. Brenda is just here fixing me some dinner. You wouldn't want her to get this wonderful lasagna all over her clothes now, would you?"

Rachel glared at Brenda, who suddenly seemed uncomfortable. She started untying the apron. "Well, I'm finished now anyway. I'll put it back."

Rachel couldn't even say anything as Mrs. Brenda scurried back into the kitchen. A few minutes later, she rushed back out. "Well, Reverend, I really must get going. I hope you enjoy your supper."

"Thank you. I sure appreciate it," Simon replied.

Brenda lingered for a moment like she wanted to say something. She finally just smiled and left.

Simon dug into his food, smiling. He slowly chewed his food like he knew Rachel was waiting on him to say something.

"Well?" Rachel finally said.

"Well what?" Simon said, pulling his napkin off his lap and dabbing at his mouth.

"You want to tell me what's going on?"

"Nope."

"Daddy."

"Brenda was just bringing me something to eat. But I know that's not what you came here to discuss."

"Can't I just come visit my daddy?"

"Sure you can. But you don't. So tell me what's going on," Simon said as he took another bite.

"Can you answer my question about Mrs. Brenda?"

"Nope." Simon chewed his food slowly.

Rachel sighed. Her father was as stubborn as they came so she knew there was no point in pressing him. She sat down, debating whether she should say anything about Lester. Finally, she decided she needed to get it off her chest.

"Lester and that church are getting on my nerves."

Simon laughed. "Why does that not surprise me?"

"I'm serious."

"I am, too." He set his fork down. "You know, Lester is a good man. He just needs you to stand tall next to him. Don't push him away."

Rachel rolled her eyes. Why in the world did she ever think her father would understand? He lived by the church, neglected his family for the church, and in the end it didn't matter because they almost voted him out anyway.

"Daddy, I'm not about to deal with any mess from Lester. Jordan's acting up. And since Lester was all caught up in church business, I made the decision myself to let him go stay with Bobby awhile."

Simon nodded. "Hmm. So you made that decision all by yourself, without consulting your husband?"

"I told you, he was too busy so I had to handle it myself."

Simon bit down on his bottom lip, like he was contemplating whether he wanted to speak. Finally, he said, "I know you 'bout to get mad at what I have to say, but you know I'm gon' tell it like it is. It's time for you to grow up."

She frowned. Her father was talking nonsense. Anybody could see how much she'd grown over the years. "Uh, I resent that. I am grown."

"Not in age. In mind," he said matter-of-factly. "Sometimes you are so wise, like your mother. But sometimes I see that same nineteen-year-old who was wreaking havoc on everyone in her path. I've seen you with your husband. You don't treat that man like you should. A man needs to feel like a man. He doesn't need his wife shooting him down and talking to him all crazy all the time. He needs his wife to support him, stand by his side. I know you didn't agree with your mother's philosophy that the man should be in charge of his household, but can you at least make him *feel* like he is?"

Surprisingly, Rachel found herself at a loss for words. When she thought about it, she knew she could be ugly to Lester

118

sometimes. It wasn't anything intentional, it was just her frustrations with that church and his commitment to it. And she was definitely having major problems with that whole submissive thing. But Lester knew she had been trying.

"Are you still pining after Bobby?" Simon asked pointedly.

Rachel's eyes grew wide. "What? Where'd that come from? Of course not. I mean, I only talk to Bobby for Jordan's sake. I love my husband. I really do."

"Who are you trying to convince? Me or yourself?"

Rachel sat in silence as her father picked up his fork and resumed eating. She let her eyes wander around the room as she took in what he said.

Rachel squinted when she saw a Royal Caribbean Cruise envelope on the end table. She walked over and picked the envelope up.

"What is this?" she asked.

"Nunya," Simon responded as he chewed his food.

"What?"

"Nunya business. Put it down."

Rachel shot her father a suspicious look and turned the envelope over. It was open so she pulled out the contents: two tickets, which read "Mr. Simon Jackson and Mrs. Brenda Bailey." Rachel looked up at her father. "You're going on a cruise with Mrs. Brenda?"

"I guess, if that's what the tickets say."

"Daddy, you can't do that."

"Why not?"

"Because . . . you're sick."

"I'm sick. Not dead. And that's all the more reason to enjoy myself while I can."

"You've got to be kidding me!"

Simon finished the last of his lasagna, then set his fork and napkin on his plate. "Rachel, have a seat." Rachel plopped down. "Aren't you the one who told me you were a mature woman?"

"And?"

"And you're acting like a spoiled child. I don't know what you think I'm supposed to do. It's been eight years since your mother died and I get very lonely."

Rachel didn't know why she was feeling this way. "I know, Daddy. It's just . . ."

"Don't you think your mother would want me to enjoy what little time I have left?"

"Don't say that."

"I'm just being real, as you young folks say." Simon weighed his words before continuing. "Rachel, you know I've never had too much to do with any woman since your mother died, but I really like Brenda. She's a sweet woman who lost her husband ten years ago. She's lonely, too. We find comfort in each other. I'm asking you to respect that."

Maybe she should be happy that her father was finally getting interested in something other than church, Rachel thought, but she just couldn't get used to the idea of her father with another woman.

"Fine, Daddy." She threw the envelope back on the table. "Date all the women you want."

Simon sighed. "Now, why you gotta be like that?"

"Because my mother devoted her life to making you happy, tending to your every need," she replied defiantly.

"How long do you think I should wait before I entertain another woman? Before I'm entitled to happiness again? Ten years? The rest of my life?"

When he said it like that, Rachel realized how stupid she sounded. Of course her father deserved to be happy. They all had their lives now. Why shouldn't he have one, too?

"You're right," she finally admitted. "I'm sorry for trippin'. I just have a lot on my mind."

"Yeah, you need to worry about your own business and stay out of mine," he joked.

Rachel grinned. "Okay, Daddy."

"Baby?"

"Yeah?"

"Go home and tend to your husband. You've neglected that boy for too long. Only so long a man can take neglect."

It was Rachel's turn to smile. "I'm not neglecting him. I admit, I may need to do better in making him feel like a man, as you say. But Lester's a different type of man. He loves me."

"Yep, more than you love him."

That was sad, but true. Rachel had hoped to fall deeply in love with him but it never came. She did love him, just nowhere near as much as she'd loved Bobby.

"Pray on it, baby girl. Ask for strength to help you nurture your husband, because while you're saying, scat, cat, someone else is around the corner saying, here kitty, kitty."

Rachel couldn't help but laugh. "Dad, where do you come up with this country stuff?"

Simon wagged his finger at her. "I'm just trying to tell you. If you don't take care of your husband, well, sooner or later, he's just gon' find someone who will. Take care of him. Because Lester may be a man of God, but he's still a man."

chapter 21

Rachel rubbed her eyes and tried to focus on the bright red numbers on her digital clock. Three A.M. Was that someone banging on her door? Lester was snoring softly and didn't seem fazed by the loud noise.

Rachel threw back the comforter and stepped out of bed. She grabbed her robe and slipped her arms in it, before making her way into the living room. Whoever was at her door was losing their mind, banging like they were crazy.

Rachel tightened the belt on her robe. "Who is it?" she called as she stood on her toes and stared out of the peephole.

"It's David! Open the door."

"Boy, what is wrong with you?" Rachel asked as she swung the door open. Then she remembered a similar scene several years ago when David had showed up at her parents' house being chased by drug dealers and quickly closed the door again. "Don't bring any of your drama up in here."

"It's Tawny!" David huffed, out of breath. "She's at the hospital about to have the baby."

"And? Shouldn't you be there with her then?" Rachel asked.

"I was on my way, but my car won't make it. It overheated as I was going down 59. I barely made it here. I need to use your car."

Rachel looked at her brother like he'd lost his mind. "Use my Benz?"

"Come on, Rachel. I need to get to the hospital."

Rachel cocked her head. She was not about to let him take her car. "I'll take you."

"Whatever, let's go." David looked like a nervous wreck.

"Can I at least just throw on some sweats?"

"Just hurry up!"

Twenty minutes later they were pulling up to Ben Taub Hospital. David barely gave the car time to stop before he barreled out. Rachel parked, then headed up to the labor and delivery unit.

She looked around for David and was directed to the NICU. He was standing in front of the window, tears in his eyes as he lightly fingered the glass. Rachel slowly walked up to him.

"Which one is yours?" Rachel softly asked.

David sounded like he was about to choke on his words. "The little boy in the middle. I have a son."

Rachel stared at the tiny brown-skinned baby with a head full of curly hair and wanted to cry herself. He looked like he couldn't weigh any more than three pounds. The baby was shaking and there were all kinds of tubes connected to him. Rachel immediately thought about Jordan and Nia when they were born. They both had been plump, healthy babies. Nothing like this. "What's wrong with him?"

"Crack," David solemnly replied. "He's a crack baby."

"Oh, my God. I thought you said Tawny was clean."

"She was, for a little while. I begged her to stop but she wouldn't. She started using again." David wiped away the tears that were running down his cheeks. "Look at him, he's so little. He's fighting for his life. And for what? Because his mama wanted to get high."

"Why is he shaking like that?"

"He's feenin', going through withdrawal."

Rachel was speechless. She had never seen her brother like this. And she had never seen a sight like this poor little baby. "What does that mean? I mean, is he going to be all right?" she asked.

David shrugged. "I don't know. I should've gotten back together with her. She begged me to take her back. At least then I could've kept an eye on her." David put one hand over his face and began sobbing.

Rachel hugged her brother. "Come on, David. This is not your fault."

He pulled away. "Yes it is. I knew how she was. I knew what

she was doing. I just didn't think about . . . about this." He turned to his son.

Rachel looked again at the baby who was now wailing like he was in excruciating pain. Even the nurse had tears in her eyes.

David swallowed and tried to regain his composure. "I named him D. J., David Jr. Tawny said she didn't care." He sniffed.

"Did you stop and see her?"

"No, I came straight here. I don't know if I can see her right now. I might hurt her." David didn't even try to mask his anger.

Rachel gently rubbed his back. She knew her brother had struggled to stay clean since their mother died. Even though she gave him a hard time, as far as she knew, he had done well. His only addiction now seemed to be to Tawny.

"I need to let the nurse know my baby's name." David put his hand on the window again before turning and heading down the hall.

A small tear trickled down Rachel's cheek as she watched her brother walk off. She turned her attention back to the baby and her heart sank. How could anything be so powerful to make a mother put her child in a position like this?

Rachel couldn't understand it, but she did know, judging from the look on her nephew's face, that he had a long, long road ahead of him. She found herself thinking the worst. What if he didn't make it? It was a thought that made her mind go back to Jordan. Yes, he'd been difficult lately, but she was so blessed to have a healthy son. Even though Jordan had only been at Bobby's for a week, seeing D. J. fighting for his life made her want to bring Jordan home, hold him, and just tell him how much she loved him.

Rachel gently put her hand on the neonatal window and said a small prayer for D. J., then headed to Bobby's to pick up her son.

chapter 22

Rachel had made up her mind, she was going to help her brother whether he wanted her to or not. She knocked on Angela's door. She knew she shouldn't be here, but this was ridiculous. If Jonathan couldn't handle his business, she would. Seeing David with D. J. had made her want to see Jonathan reunited with his son even more.

Besides, devoting her energy to her brothers' lives would help her forget about her own troubles. She'd brought Jordan home two days ago—against his will—but she wanted him with her. Besides, Bobby seemed like he had a lot of stuff on his mind and Jordan wasn't doing anything over there but playing video games. Both Rachel and Lester had sat down and talked to Jordan about his behavior and the very next day he went to his new school and got into a fight. She had an appointment with the counselor tomorrow. Hopefully, they'd be able to get to the root of Jordan's problems.

Right now, though, she was going to do whatever she could to get Jonathan and his son together.

Angela slowly opened the door, staring at Rachel suspiciously.

"Hello, Angela," Rachel said.

"Hello, Rachel."

"May I come in?" Rachel asked. She was going to try to be reasonable, appeal to Angela as a mother.

"I'm just about to head out."

Rachel gently pushed past her and walked inside. "This won't take but a minute."

Angela sighed and closed the door. "Look, Rachel, if you're here to argue your brother's case, don't bother. I'm not changing my mind."

"Angela, have you prayed about this?" Rachel wanted Angela to see that she was sincere. "I know you are a deeply spiritual woman—or you used to be, at least. I'm sure if you ask God for guidance, He will show you that what you're doing is not right."

"And what your brother is doing *is* right?"

"I know Jonathan hurt you, but one of the core issues in the Bible is forgiveness." Rachel sat down in the wingback chair in the living room.

Angela looked at Rachel like she was crazy. "My sister told me you were a first lady, but you'll have to excuse me if I have a hard time sitting here listening to you spout the word of God."

"Do you still have a relationship with God?"

"Huh? What does that have to do with anything?"

"Because if you did, you would see what you're doing isn't right."

"*Isn't right?* You want to talk to me about right? Talk to your gay brother."

Rachel fidgeted in her seat. "While I don't condone Jonathan's lifestyle, he's still my family; there's nothing I can do about that. It's not up to me to judge him."

"Well, you can turn the other cheek all you want, but I can't do it." Angela sat down across from Rachel. "You married Lester Adams, right?"

"That's correct. He's the pastor at Zion Hill now."

"So can you honestly say to me that if you found out Lester was gay, you'd wish him well and go on about your merry business?"

Rachel almost laughed. She'd kill that fool dead. But that was beside the point. "I'm not talking about what-ifs. I'm talking about reality. And the reality is that Jonathan has as much right to see his son as you do."

Angela stood. "It's obvious you will never understand my decision. But it is *my* decision."

Rachel stood as well. "I'm trying to stop this before it goes to court. Before things get ugly."

Angela spun around with such an evil look on her face Rachel couldn't believe it. "Rachel, honey. If Jonathan tries to get his grimy little paws on my child, I'm going to show him what ugly really is," she spat.

Rachel stepped closer. "Let me warn you, Angela. At one time, I was the baby mama from hell. I know all the tricks in the book. My family and I will pray real hard that this works out—then do whatever it takes to make sure it does. My brother *will* see his child. By any means necessary."

Angela didn't look fazed. "Consider me warned. And let me warn you." She pointed an impeccably manicured finger at Rachel. "You and the rest of that Jackson clan have no idea who you're messing with. My family can get in the gutter, too."

Rachel nodded. Angela had gotten a little spunk in her over the years. "I will advise you to seriously think about what you're doing."

"Thought about it. Stand by it. Now, get out of my house."

Though Rachel smiled at Angela as she made her way out, she knew that from the looks of things, Jonathan getting joint custody wasn't going to be easy.

chapter 23

Too bad you can't choose your family. Angela watched everybody arguing at her parents' kitchen table. She knew they were all just trying to help, but honestly, they were getting on her last nerve. Her parents; her brother, Darryl; her cousin, Buster; and Buster's mother, Mrs. Brooks's sister Georgia, were gathered in the kitchen talking about ways to keep Jonathan from getting any time with Chase.

"Look, we only need one person to talk at a time," her father said, trying to regain control of the family meeting. "Now, Buster, you said you have a plan."

"Excuse me," Mrs. Brooks interrupted. "You all didn't give me a chance to finish detailing my plan."

Angela sighed. "Mother, for the one-hundredth time, we are not going to frame Jonathan for murder."

"Why can't we frame him?" Mrs. Brooks asked. "That way, he'd get sent to prison or something for a very long time."

"Well, Ma, there's just one problem with your plan," Darryl interjected.

"What?"

"We'd have to actually murder somebody first."

Mrs. Brooks just stared blankly at Darryl. "Well, I didn't say I had worked out all the details."

Mr. Brooks shook his head. "Buster, I hope you have a better plan than your aunt here. We've had the private investigator following that boy for weeks and nothing. All he does is go to work, then to his father's house, then back home."

"I wouldn't be surprised if he was holding someone captive in his apartment. That's why he doesn't go anywhere or do anything. They're probably tied up in a closet or something, or maybe chopped up in the freezer," Mrs. Brooks muttered.

Angela stared at her mother. *Where does she come up with this stuff?*

"Look," Buster said, "I already got it under control. One of my boys will handle this."

"Oooohhhh, you gonna rough Jonathan up?" Mrs. Brooks asked, a little too eagerly. "Send him a severed thumb as a message?"

"Lynn, no more *Sopranos* for you," Mr. Brooks said. Angela was glad somebody was trying to be a voice of reason, because her mother was totally going off the deep end. "Besides, even if we do rough him up, how will that stop him from still trying to see Chase when he gets better?"

"Would y'all let Buster finish telling us what his plan is?" Aunt Georgia said. "Since y'all didn't like my idea just to say Chase wasn't his."

"Because you want us to make my child out to be some kind of slut who sleeps around and doesn't know who her baby's daddy is! I don't think so," Mrs. Brooks snapped.

"Plus, DNA would quickly nip that plan in the bud," Mr. Brooks added.

"Would y'all just listen?" Buster said. "I told you I have a plan."

Angela leaned back in her chair. Buster had done hard time for armed robbery, so he definitely had all the connections to do something illegal.

"As I was saying," Buster continued, "my boy got some hook-ups. He can get some people to drug Jonathan, then arrange some pictures for y'all to give the judge."

Drugs? Angela wasn't sure she wanted to go there. What if something happened and he overdosed? She would never be able to live with herself.

"Look," she said, rising from her seat. "Why do we have to have a plan in the first place? Can't we just have faith in the system?"

"The same system that acquitted O.J. just because the glove didn't fit?" Mrs. Brooks snapped.

"They acquitted the Juice because he didn't do it," Mr. Brooks snapped back defensively. "It was a setup if I ever seen one."

"Mmm-hmm, that's why he wrote a book called *If I Did It*," Mrs. Brooks mumbled.

"If!" Mr. Brooks responded. "*If* he had done it. Not I did it!"

"Helll-ooo," Angela said, waving her hands. "Can we stay focused and not digress?"

Buster leaned in toward his mother. "What do 'digress' mean?"

Angela took a deep breath. "This is ridiculous. I can handle Jonathan on my own. I don't need a plan. I don't need anyone to do anything to him. Yet, anyway. I thought I wanted to play dirty, but I just want this to be over with." She plopped back down in her seat.

"Baby, sometimes desperate times call for desperate measures. And these are desperate times," her father said sternly.

"I understand that, but this . . . this is all making my head hurt." Angela rubbed her temples.

"Well, sweetie, you go lie down," Mrs. Brooks said. "We'll figure out a plan. Come to think of it, it's probably better you don't know what's going down anyway."

Angela stared at her mother, who had turned into someone she didn't recognize. She then turned her attention to her other family members. They were all taking a sick pleasure in plotting Jonathan's demise.

Watching all of them sitting there, hatching their evil plots, made Angela wonder if her whole quest to keep Chase away from his father was going to spiral into something she would end up regretting.

chapter 24

"Earth to Rachel."

Rachel snapped out of her thoughts as Lester waved his hand in her face. She had tuned him out to replay her conversation with Angela in her head. She'd been wracking her brain trying to come up with a way to beat her ex-sister-in-law at her own game.

"Oh, I'm sorry. What were you saying?" she said.

Lester exhaled in frustration. "Where is your mind? I've been trying to talk to you about us for the last week and you never seem to be all there."

"What is it you want to talk about, Lester?" After her little talk with her father, Rachel knew she needed to check the attitude and show her husband a little more attention, but she had a lot on her mind right now.

"Us. I have some major issues that I would like to discuss." Lester walked over and sat down on the edge of the bed. Rachel was sitting up against the headboard, her laptop in her lap.

"Everything is major with you, Lester." Rachel flipped open her computer. Maybe if she Googled Angela she would find something she'd done in the last seven years that they could use against her.

Lester reached up and slammed her laptop shut. She looked at him like he'd lost his mind. "What is your problem?"

"Rachel, I'm trying to talk to you. I'm trying to tell you the problems I'm having with our marriage." Lester exhaled. "The problems I'm having with you."

"Oh, so you're having problems with me?" Rachel cut her eyes at him. "What did I do wrong this time?" She was definitely about to get an attitude now. Since the First Ladies Council meeting, she really had been trying to do better at church. She'd gotten rid of the Baby Phat outfits and dressed a lot more conservatively. She'd been nicer to people at church; some of them had even noticed. But with all that she'd done, Lester obviously still wasn't satisfied.

He stared at her, then finally said, "Why do I bother?" He walked out of the room.

Rachel jumped up and followed him. "I don't know. Why *do* you bother? I mean, I'm not a proper first lady. I can't keep my son in line. Your beloved congregation can't stand me. Whatever do you see in me?"

He turned to face her. "I saw a woman I wanted to love for

the rest of her life. A woman who won't let me love her," he said in a serious tone.

"What is that supposed to mean?" Rachel folded her arms. "How am I stopping you from loving me?"

"Just forget it, Rachel."

"Yeah, Lester. Let's just forget it because you're talking nonsense." She returned to the bed and popped her laptop open. "I'm trying to help my brother keep his child!" she yelled. "I don't have time to deal with minor stuff like this."

He reappeared in the doorway. "Oh, so our marriage is minor now?"

She looked up at him, exasperated. "Good night, Lester."

He stared at her, then turned and walked out without responding. Rachel ignored the sound of the front door slamming as she logged on to Google.

chapter 25

Jonathan set the bottle down and bounced D.J. on his shoulder as he paced around the den. He had tried everything—the bottle, changing his diaper, singing to him. Nothing was working.

Jonathan thought it would be great having a baby around since he'd missed out on his own son's infant years, but D.J. wouldn't stop crying. Jonathan wanted to scream. The baby had been home two weeks and David appeared to be going just as crazy.

Jonathan looked at his father, who was rocking gently in his recliner reading the newspaper.

"How can you sit there so calmly with D.J. screaming the way he is?" Jonathan asked.

Simon smiled. "I just tune him out."

"Here, why don't you take him? Maybe you can get him to settle down." Jonathan held out the baby.

Simon folded his paper, stood up, and rubbed the baby's chin. "Nope," he said. "I've served my time. I'm done raising babies." He smiled as he headed toward the stairs.

"But, I mean, you've done this before. You know what to do."

"No, I don't. You know your mama took care of you all as babies. So I couldn't help you if I wanted to. Gots to go now. Brenda will be here in a bit. We're going to Pastor Vaughn's anniversary celebration at Mt. Sinai in Port Arthur. Have fun." Simon headed up the steps before Jonathan could protest.

Jonathan looked down at D.J., who was now sniffling wearily. Jonathan felt so sorry for the poor guy. He peered out the window. David and Tawny were still outside arguing. David looked furious and Tawny was once again standing there with a stupid grin on her face.

She had shown up more than an hour ago, demanding to see D. J. Her eyes were bloodshot, her hair was disheveled, and she smelled like she hadn't bathed in days. David had asked her to come back when she wasn't high and she'd gone ballistic. They'd taken the argument outside and had been there ever since.

Jonathan glanced down at the baby again. He'd finally worn himself out and was now sound asleep. Jonathan breathed a sigh of relief, then eased over to the bassinet to lay him down.

He had just covered D.J. up when Tawny came busting through the patio door. David was close on her heels.

"Tawny, we are not finished talking," he said.

"Yes, we are," she replied. She looked around the room. "Where's my baby's bags?"

"I told you, the only way you will get my child is over my dead body," David said defiantly.

"Then you 'bout to be one dead mother—"

"Would you two shut up?" Jonathan interrupted. "D.J. just fell asleep. Can't you have some consideration for a change?"

Tawny looked at Jonathan like he was crazy. "Consider this. Gimme my kid or I'm calling the cops. In case you forgot, I'm his mama."

David rubbed his forehead, no doubt trying to calm down. "Look, Tawny, please don't do this. You don't even want him. And besides, you don't have any place to take him."

"He goes where I go."

"On the street?"

"So? You ain't too much better living up here with your daddy." She looked at Jonathan. "Big ol' forty-year-old man, living with his daddy." She reached into the bassinet.

David grabbed her arm before she touched the baby. "Okay, you win. I'll get it."

Tawny smiled. "I thought you'd see things my way."

Jonathan looked back and forth between the two of them, a confused look across his face. "Get what, David?"

Tawny's mood seemed to suddenly change. She was chipper and grinning from ear to ear. "That's between me and your brother," she said, never taking her eyes off David. "So go get it."

"Come on, Tawny. I'm going to need some time."

"I ain't got time," she said sharply.

"Tawny, you're being unreasonable."

She rolled her eyes. "Fine," she huffed. "Gimme what you got. And don't even front 'cause today is Friday and I know you got paid. I want it all." She held out her hand.

"Tawny, my check wasn't but six hundred dollars. I need to buy diapers and milk."

"Waaah, waaah, waaah. Get your old man or your brother here to give you some money. Gimme it all or me and D. J. are outta here." She folded her arms and turned up her lips.

"I don't believe you," David mumbled as he pulled out his wallet. He pulled out five crisp one-hundred-dollar bills. "Here," he said, slamming the money into her hand. "I'm keeping a hundred because I have to take care of our child since you seem to have no desire to."

Tawny smiled as she took the money and stuffed it in her bra. "You trying to make me feel guilty? Sorry, boo. Ain't gonna work. You the one who wanted to play proud papa and everything."

Jonathan looked on, dumbfounded. Tawny couldn't be serious. No mother could be that cruel.

"So, you gon' have the rest of the money next week?" she asked eagerly.

"I will do everything in my power to get it," David said dejectedly.

"That's my boo." She looked at the baby while nervously shaking, no doubt feenin' for her next fix. "You see what lengths your daddy will go to," Tawny cooed. She looked at David, who was scowling at her. "What? I told you just this one time and I'm done. I'll sign over rights to you and everything."

"Don't mess with me, Tawny," David warned.

"Or what? You know you done gone soft on me." Tawny playfully poked David in the stomach. "Stop being so sensitive. Well, I'm out," she said, heading toward the door. "I'll see you in a week."

Jonathan and David watched Tawny prance out of the front door. Silence hung in the air before Jonathan turned to his brother. "Please tell me you are not about to really try and buy her off."

David walked over and took the bottle off the coffee table. "Please tell me what other choice I have," he said as he walked into the kitchen and dropped the bottle in the sink.

Jonathan followed, taking note how his father kept the kitchen as immaculate as his mother had when she was alive. "Why don't you try going to social services, or filing for custody?"

David shot his brother a crazy look. "Yeah, right. I've been to rehab, what four, five times. I have a criminal record and I'm a black man. Sure, a judge would just love to rule in my favor."

"You can at least try," Jonathan tried to reason.

"No, the judge will just end up putting the baby in foster care, then neither of us will have him. I can't take that chance."

"If you give Tawny money, you know she's just gon' keep coming back for more."

"I'm just gon' have to take my chances. I told her it was a one-time thing and she said I could find an attorney and she'd sign over her rights if I gave her the money." There were stress lines all across David's face.

Jonathan sighed, sensing that his brother's mind was made up. "How much does she want?"

"Ten grand." David said as he opened the refrigerator, pulled out a can of Coke and popped the top.

"What?" Jonathan asked. "You're kidding me, right?"

David took a long gulp of the soda. "I wish I was. She wants ten grand or else she's going to take D. J. The bad part is she doesn't even want him—but she knows I do, so she's just using him to hustle me for money."

"Dang, that's deep. So what you gon' do?" Jonathan sat down at the table.

"I'm gonna give her the money," David replied as he sat down across from his brother.

"And just where are you going to get that kind of money?"

"I still have about five left over from Mama's insurance policy. I'll just have to get the rest from this cat I know."

Jonathan narrowed his eyes. "Is this *cat* some of the old people you used to run with?"

David ignored Jonathan as he took another sip of his Coke.

"David, are you sure you don't want to go through the courts? They'll give you custody."

"Man, I don't have time for that! She's right. She's his legal guardian. And I don't want my baby out on that street one day with her so I'm gonna do what I have to do."

"But you can't go hooking back up with those people."

David slammed the soda down. "Look, Jon, don't start preaching to me, a'ight? I'm gon' do whatever I have to do to keep my son away from Tawny."

Jonathan could tell by the determined look on his brother's face there was nothing he could say or do to keep David from getting that money. He just hoped it wasn't a decision David would live to regret.

chapter 26

The First Ladies Council meetings were working. Linda Morgan had become a praying partner and Rachel found herself garnering a lot of strength from the ease with which Sister Morgan handled things. Whenever she felt herself getting weak, she'd call Linda, the two of them would pray, and Rachel would find her attitude immediately improving. And she'd been doing well. In fact, two members had brought her a fresh-baked pound cake, saying they noticed "a change and just wanted to compliment" her.

Still, today she was happy to see the services wrapping up. Jordan had a big science project due tomorrow and she didn't want to be up all night helping him with it. He'd actually been doing so much better in school since he began meeting with his counselor three times a week. For some reason, Jordan was harboring a lot of anger and the counselor was helping him work through it.

Lester waited for the music to die down before he started calling people to the front to join the church. This always had been Rachel's least favorite part of the Sunday service. It could drag on for another thirty minutes. Thankfully, only three people came to join the Christian experience. A fourth person, a leggy, golden-haired white woman said she wanted to make a testimony.

Rachel thought she pretty much knew everyone in Zion Hill, but this woman didn't look the least bit familiar. Rachel considered shooting her husband a look to remind him that they had cut out the testimony part of service, but something about the woman intrigued her.

"Giving honor to God, Pastor Adams, deacons, family, and friends," the church secretary, Tricia Yancy, began. "We have before us today Miss Mary Richardson. She comes today to give a testimony and request prayer."

Sister Yancy handed the microphone to Miss Richardson, who smiled at her before stepping in front of the congregation.

Rachel took in the woman's appearance. She was actually quite stunning, with her shoulder-length blonde hair, gray eyes, and slender frame. Still, even though they did have visitors of other races from time to time, today Mary was the only one.

"Ummmm, hello," the woman began, her voice soft and fragile. "I just wanted to come before you all today to ask you to pray for me." The woman took a deep breath. "The devil is at work on me. I don't know any way to say this other than to come right out and say it. I am having an affair with a married man." Several women in the sanctuary groaned, including Rachel. Mary lowered her head in shame, took a deep breath, then looked back out at the congregation. "I know I was wrong, but I am weak. I love him with all of my heart. He claims that he still loves his wife. But he constantly turns to me because she doesn't appreciate him and after seven years of marriage, I think his love is wavering. He wants to build a life with me and I want one with him, but I know he doesn't want to hurt his wife."

Rachel shook her head. *Just scandalous,* she thought. *Why in the world would that woman stand up in front of the church and put her business out there like that?*

The woman dabbed at her eyes. "Part of me wants to ask that you pray he finds the strength to leave his wife and be with me, but I know that is not the right thing to do. So I stand before you today to ask that you pray for me, pray that God gives me the strength to rebuke the devil and do what I know is right and walk away. I'm coming to you in the open like this because I believe there is a power in prayer and this is a battle I cannot win alone. Thank you." She took another deep breath and handed the microphone back to Sister Yancy.

Rachel could not believe her eyes. The congregation was on its feet applauding this woman. They should be throwing stones at her, not standing up there clapping for her and saying, "We're praying for you, Sister." They needed to be praying for the wife of whoever's home she was breaking up. Rachel was all for forgiveness—she'd learned that much over the years—but not when it came to some woman openly messing with a married man.

Lester took his place back at the podium. He had the congregation bow their heads and say a quick prayer. "Blessings, Sister," he told the woman after they were done. "You will be in our prayers."

The woman slowly nodded as she returned to her seat, tears flowing down her cheeks.

Lester wrapped up the church service and made his rounds greeting members on their way out. Afterward, he met back up with Rachel in his office.

"So, what's for dinner?" he asked as he loosened his tie.

"I thought maybe we could go out to eat." Rachel stood and walked over to kiss her husband. Unfortunately, she still hadn't mastered the art of Sunday cooking like her mother had. Loretta would've died rather than go out to eat on Sunday.

"Come on, sweetheart. I really could use a good, home-cooked meal."

"Me, too. That's why I suggest Mikki's Café. You know their oxtails are delicious." Rachel smiled.

Lester shook his head. "Let's just go to my grandmother's. She's cooking—"

"Don't even think about it."

He sighed in defeat. "I'll grab the kids. Mikki's it is."

Rachel ignored the look of frustration on his face. "So what did you think of that floozy today?" Rachel asked while she stood waiting for him to gather some papers off his desk.

"What floozy?"

"The floozy who got up in church and told everybody how she was sleeping with a married man."

"Maybe she was trying to redeem herself. The Lord reaches out to sinners from all walks." Lester never looked up as he sifted through the papers on his desk.

Rachel crossed her arms as she sat down. "Hmmph. She gets no sympathy from me. I hope her no-good lover's wife catches him and castrates him."

Lester smiled. "Ouch! Must you be so graphic?"

"I just can't stand cheating men or the women they cheat with." Lester shot her a funny look. Rachel knew exactly what he was thinking. "And you can't even compare me to that woman. Number one, I was eighteen years old when I cheated on Bobby; and number two, I was not married. The rules change once you say 'I do,'" she said defensively. She might have done a lot of things wrong in the past, but she believed in being faithful to your husband.

Lester smirked. "I didn't say a word."

"Whatever." Rachel threw her hands up, stood, and headed to the door.

"May I ask why you're mad at me?" Lester said.

"Can we just go, please?" Rachel tucked her purse underneath her arm and stood by the door tapping her foot.

Lester stepped toward her and put his arm around her waist. "Come on, baby, don't be like that." He leaned in to kiss her. Rachel turned her cheek.

"I'm not being like anything. You're the one who wanted to turn this conversation back around on me."

"I don't understand how this turned into us arguing," Lester said with a sigh.

Rachel put her hands on her hips. "So tell the truth. Do you condone what she did?"

Lester exhaled. "Rachel, it is not my place to judge. It is only my place to welcome her into the Word of God. I didn't judge you and I'm not going to judge her."

Rachel rolled her eyes. "Oh, so I'm in the same category as her because of something I did ten years ago?"

"Good grief! Why must you make everything out to be so dramatic?"

She caught herself before going off. She wasn't in the mood to argue. "You know what, Lester? Forget I said anything. Let's just go get something to eat and go home. I need to help Jordan with his project. Plus, Jonathan has his court hearing in the morning and I want to have my mind right for that."

"I'll go get the kids," Lester softly replied.

"I'll be in the car." A small smile crossed Rachel's face as she headed to her car. She was so proud of how she'd taken the high road in that argument. If that didn't show she was making progress, nothing would.

chapter 27

Jonathan tried to shake off his nervousness. Today was the day of reckoning. He was about to go before a judge who would determine whether his future would include his son. The attorney Jonathan had hired—a fierce, white-haired, fifty-something woman—was confident that they would emerge victorious.

"The judge is ready for us," Claudia Van Buren said as she stuck her head out of the courtroom.

Rachel slipped her fingers through her brother's and they followed Claudia inside. Simon and David were right behind them.

Angela, her family, and what seemed like her entire neighborhood were already seated on the opposite side of the courtroom. While Angela didn't look their way, almost everyone else scowled as the Jacksons walked by.

Forever the diplomat, Simon eased over to their side of the courtroom.

"Afternoon, Brother Brooks," Simon said.

Angela's father glared at him and didn't reply. David grabbed Simon's arm and led him over to the bench behind Jonathan and his attorney.

Jonathan stared at Angela, who seemed like she had been crying. She caught Jonathan looking at her and shot him an evil glare.

Jonathan turned his attention to Rachel, who was staring at the judge's bench. He knew she was recalling being in this same courtroom eight years ago, trying to convince a judge not to let Bobby have joint custody of Jordan.

That case had gone terribly wrong: The judge had told Rachel she'd better be grateful Bobby hadn't asked for full custody because he would've gotten it.

"All rise. The honorable Vincent Rosenthal presiding," the bailiff announced as the judge, who looked like he had just stepped off a tanning bed, walked in and sat down.

"You may be seated," the judge said as he began reviewing a folder for a minute before glancing up. "Are both parties ready to get started?"

Both attorneys stood and announced, "We are."

Judge Rosenthal nodded. "Well, Mr. Slade," he said, turning his attention to Angela's attorney. "We'll begin with you."

Her attorney, a no-nonsense-looking black man with just

enough gray hair to make him distinguished, walked around to the front of the table. "Your Honor, I am not one to stand in judgment of others. Nor is my client. Although the Bible clearly states its position on homosexuality, we recognize that times are changing. We don't knock anyone who chooses alternative lifestyles. Where we do begin to have a problem is when that lifestyle is forced onto my client's child."

Jonathan looked on in disgust. He couldn't believe they were making this case about that. What about parenting skills? Why couldn't they give him a chance to show them he would be a good parent? He wanted to scream as the attorney rambled on about how Angela had to bear the burden of raising Chase alone all these years. Jonathan pulled Claudia's arm, trying to get her to object or something, when Mr. Slade started talking about how vulnerable Chase was and how being exposed to Jonathan and his "many lovers" would negatively impact the child.

Jonathan glanced over at Rachel, who was squirming in her seat. He knew she was trying hard not to put her two cents in.

Jonathan let out a sigh when Angela's attorney finally sat down. He leaned in and whispered to Claudia, "Can you please let the judge know I am not like that? That I am from a good, Christian family and that this is not about my sexuality?"

Claudia patted his arm. "Let me do my job," she said.

Jonathan felt better as his attorney took center stage and described him as a father who desperately wanted a relationship with his son. She even produced pages of testimony from children of gay parents stating that their parents' sexuality didn't have a negative impact on them. She also presented copies of all the money orders and checks Jonathan had sent over the years. Jonathan was so happy he had listened to Rachel and had kept copies of everything.

"So Your Honor, we ask that you do not deny Chase his God-given right—the right to know his father." Claudia closed her folder and returned to her seat.

Jonathan smiled as she sat down. The courtroom was quiet as the judge studied some papers in front of him. "We will take a break for lunch and I'll return at one P.M. with my ruling. Parties are dismissed," he said.

Lunch? Why did they have to wait through lunch? Jonathan stood while the judge left the courtroom. He looked over at Angela's family as they swarmed around her. You'd have thought he was trying to get full custody of his son. All he wanted was the right to see Chase.

Angela was softly weeping. Jonathan couldn't help it, he had to say something. "Angela," he said, walking toward her. "I'm so sorry. I never wanted to hurt you. I never wanted it to come to this."

"Look, you little punk," Mr. Brooks said as he stepped in front of his daughter, "hurting her is all you've done since you met her."

Simon quickly interjected, "Come on, Brother Brooks. Why don't we let the young people handle this?"

"No disrespect, Reverend Jackson, because you know I have always thought highly of you, but your son has caused my daughter a lifetime of pain and I'm not about to stand around and watch him add to it by trying to take her child." Mr. Brooks's pale complexion was turning crimson with his anger.

"I'm not trying to take him. I just want to see him," Jonathan pleaded.

"And teach him what, pray tell?" Mrs. Brooks said. "Morals? Values?"

Rachel stepped in. "Look, there is no need for you to attack my brother. I don't understand why we can't handle this in a dignified manner."

"What? Now the town tramp is trying to be dignified?" Mrs. Brooks snapped.

Angela covered her eyes. "Stop it! Everybody please just stop it," she cried.

The courtroom grew silent. Angela looked up. "May I please speak to Jonathan alone?"

Mrs. Brooks looked at her daughter in shock. "You can't be serious. There is nothing for you to talk to him about."

"Mother, please," Angela groaned.

Simon extended his hand toward the door. "Why don't all of us wait outside while they talk."

Rachel and David led the way out. Mr. and Mrs. Brooks sighed before reluctantly leaving the courtroom. "We're right outside, baby," Mrs. Brooks said as she left.

Jonathan wished he could rewind time and make all of this go away. He could see the hurt in Angela's eyes, pain not just from the custody fight, but from everything he had put her through.

"Why are you doing this? Why can't you just leave us alone?" Angela said.

"Angela, I am so sorry. I know I hurt you. I tried to leave you and Chase alone and just provide financial support. But I couldn't. I just want to see my son."

Angela wiped away the tears that had begun flowing down her face. "Can I ask you something?"

"Anything, Angela. Anything at all."

"Why did you marry me?"

Jonathan looked in her eyes. "Because I knew you were the best woman a man could ever ask for. The best woman a man could ever want."

"Only you didn't want a woman. Either that or I wasn't woman enough for you," she said as if she had established it as a fact years ago.

"I was so confused. I knew how people wanted me to be. I knew what I was supposed to be. But my heart wouldn't cooperate. I thought if I married you, the perfect woman, all of those horrible, confusing feelings would go away."

"I was your guinea pig?" She was desperately searching for answers.

"You were not a guinea pig." Jonathan rubbed his forehead. He was trying to fight off tears himself.

She suddenly straightened, her expression hardening. "So you think it's wise that I let my seven-year-old son come around you and your boyfriend?"

"First of all, it's *our* seven-year-old son. And second of all, I don't have a boyfriend anymore."

Angela looked stunned. "I thought you two were so in love."

"This isn't about Tracy, or anyone else for that matter. It's about us and our child."

Angela was still taking in the news that he was no longer with Tracy. "Jonathan, you destroyed our marriage, our future, for your little boyfriend and you're not even together now?" Her voice was laced with anger.

Jonathan let out a deep breath. "Please, can we only talk about our child?"

"No, we cannot, Jonathan. That's what this whole custody battle is about. You chose your lover over your child, over our life. Now that he's gone, you want us back in your life. You have lost your mind."

Any progress they'd been making was gone. Angela walked out of the courtroom.

chapter 28

It seemed like the judge had taken forever to reconvene, but now that they were back in the courtroom, Jonathan felt like the walls were closing in. His heart was beating rapidly and he was sweating profusely. He just wanted this all to be over with.

Both families were back in their seats. Jonathan and Angela looked on anxiously as the judge took his place behind the bench. He studied his papers and wrote something on his notepad before looking up at the attorneys.

Jonathan glanced over at a glossy-eyed Angela. She was staring straight ahead as if she were in a trance. Her parents sat behind her, scowling.

"Just because we no longer like the person we chose to have

a child with does not mean, legally, that we have the right to cut that individual out of the child's life," the judge began.

Angela's shoulders sank, but she kept her head high.

"After careful consideration," Judge Rosenthal continued, "the petitioner's request for visitation for his son is granted."

Angela let out a loud gasp as she slumped in her chair.

"I am also granting the mother's request for supervised visitation for a period of six months."

Jonathan looked at his attorney. Supervised? What did they think he was, a serial killer or something? He wouldn't be able to see his child without someone watching his every move?

Claudia stood up. "Your Honor, please. My client is no threat to anyone. He comes from a nice, stable, Christian home."

Mrs. Brooks suddenly launched into a loud coughing attack.

Claudia shot her a sideways glance and continued. "Mr. Jackson has been denied the opportunity to see his son for seven years. He shouldn't be punished further by being treated as a danger to his own child—for no reason, might I add."

Mrs. Brooks stood up and yelled, "Don't leave him alone with that boy! You don't know what he'll do to Chase. He was probably molested as a child, that's why he's the way he is!"

Angela buried her face in her hands. Mr. Brooks grabbed his wife's hand and tried to pull her back down. Jonathan shook his head in frustration.

"Order in the court!" Judge Rosenthal banged his gavel. "Ma'am"—he pointed at Mrs. Brooks—"another outburst like that and I will not only have you thrown out of this courtroom, but thrown in jail."

Mrs. Brooks jerked her arm away from her husband, shot Jonathan a vicious look, then sat back down.

The judge turned back to Claudia. "Counselor, your concerns are duly noted. I will allow unsupervised visits, but no overnights pending further review. We will review the progress of this arrangement in three months. A suitable visitation schedule will be worked out with a court-appointed caseworker. Court is adjourned."

Jonathan wanted to turn a backflip. He hugged Claudia as his family gathered around him. Everyone was smiling as they congratulated him. But as Jonathan watched Angela's family console her as she sobbed he couldn't help but feel his victory was bittersweet.

chapter 29

It had been a good week, but Rachel had a feeling that that was all about to change. She'd gotten out of going to Lester's grandmother's the previous Sunday, so she knew she was going to have to go today. She didn't put up a fight when Lester announced they were having dinner at Naomi's, and even now, she tried to keep a positive attitude. But Nia and Jordan were driving her crazy with their incessant arguing. She turned around in the front seat of the car and yelled, "Sit your behinds down, before I beat you into next week!"

Jordan rolled his eyes. Nia pouted before leaning back in her seat. "No fair, Jordan started it," she said.

Rachel sighed as she rubbed her temples. It was bad enough that she had to go deal with Lester's grandmother;

no, she had to deal with Nia and Jordan fighting all the way there, too.

"Rachel, are you okay?" Lester asked, rubbing her leg.

"I'm fine."

"I'm sorry I asked you to come," he said.

Rachel tried to smile at her husband. She wanted to tell him that he hadn't asked, but she decided to leave well enough alone. "No, I'm sorry. I'm fine. Let's just try to have an enjoyable dinner."

Lester's expression told her he was grateful she was trying to compromise.

As soon as they pulled in the driveway, Naomi opened the door, clad in her signature ruffled dress, this one in black, with a white lace collar. She had that same dress in every color.

Naomi smiled widely at Lester as he made his way into the house. Of course, her smile faded when Rachel walked in, but it reappeared when Jordan and Nia entered.

Although she couldn't stand Naomi, Rachel had to admit that the woman treated Jordan and Nia like they were her own flesh and blood. In fact, she spoiled them rotten.

"Hi, Grandma Naomi," Nia sang as she kissed Naomi on the cheek.

Naomi held her arms out to hug both kids. "Look at my babies. I just don't get to see y'all enough."

Rachel knew that was a dig at her but she ignored it.

"And Jordan, you just turning into a regular little man." She pinched his cheek.

"What's up, Grandma Naomi?" Jordan half smiled. At least he wasn't growling like he normally did.

"You know I have some tea cakes and your favorite Play-Station games waiting for you in the den."

"They don't need tea cakes," Rachel said. "It's right before dinner."

"Nonsense." Naomi waved the kids away. "Go on, the tea cakes are in the back."

Jordan and Nia smiled before taking off.

Rachel bit down on her lip. It was going to be a long day.

"Rachel, I thought Lester said you were trying to lose weight," Naomi said as she made her way into the kitchen. She popped Rachel on the behind as she passed. "What are you now, a size twenty?"

Rachel cut her eyes at Lester. She was a size eight and this woman knew it! "Mrs. Naomi, I didn't come over here to be insul—"

Lester cut her off. "Grandma, what'd you cook?"

"Ohh, baby, I cooked your favorite. Smothered pork chops." She walked through the swinging doors into the kitchen.

Rachel hit Lester in the arm. "You better get your grandmother under control before I tell her old behind something," she hissed.

"Please, baby. Don't create a scene. You know how she is."

This was one area she and Lester definitely didn't see eye to eye on. He let his grandmother say and do whatever she wanted. "I do know how she is, Lester. And I know I'm not about to sit up here and let her talk to me any kind of way. I am not in the mood to be ridiculed by her today," she whispered fiercely.

"Rachel, why is it so difficult for you to get along with my grandmother?"

Rachel put a finger to her chin. "Ummm, let's see. She disrespects my parenting and my cooking and calls me fat . . ." Rachel looked at her watch. "All that in less than five minutes. Should I go on?"

"She's old, Rachel. And sickly."

"That doesn't give her the right to be just plain evil."

They walked into the kitchen and sat at the white ceramic kitchen table. *This is what happens when I try to compromise, be a good wife. It's not appreciated and I end up getting treated like crap.*

Naomi checked on dinner, then sat down across from Lester and started talking to him like Rachel wasn't even in the room.

"So, baby," she said, "you did a wonderful job on that sermon this morning. I thought I was gon' get the Holy Ghost."

Rachel tried not to make a face. So what else was new? She got the Holy Ghost every Sunday.

"I saw Jackie Long yesterday. She told me to tell you hello." Naomi had an innocent look on her face. Rachel could tell the old woman was just trying to get under her skin by bringing up Lester's ex-girlfriend.

Before Lester could respond, Rachel stood up. "If you all will excuse me, I'm going to the bathroom."

She left the table, ignoring the apologetic look in Lester's eyes.

Rachel made her way down the long hallway, which was covered with photos from every single year of Lester's life. Naomi had raised him since his parents died in a car wreck and she doted on him like he was the Second Coming.

After Rachel used the bathroom, she stuck her head in the den to check on the kids, then headed back to the kitchen. She was determined not to let Naomi get to her. For Lester's sake, she would try to tolerate her for the next hour or so. After they ate dinner, though, they were going to have to leave.

"—unequally yoked, that's what y'all are."

Rachel stopped just outside the kitchen to hear what Naomi was talking about.

"Grandma, I've told you, I love Rachel. She's my soul mate," Lester protested. Rachel was glad to hear him finally stand up to his grandmother as far as she was concerned.

"You remember when that guest preacher from Lily Grove preached about being unequally yoked?" she said. "He said fearing singleness breeds insanity. You didn't want to be alone, so you hooked up with her. That's insane."

"Grandma, please." Lester sighed.

"Don't please me. Please God. Deuteronomy twenty-two ten clearly says 'Do not plow with an ox and a donkey.'"

"What is that supposed to mean?"

"You're the preacher. You know what it means. You're an ox. Your wife in there is a donkey. You just can't make it work no matter how much you try," Naomi said matter-of-factly.

Rachel had heard enough. She refused to spend one more minute in this woman's house. She went back to the den. "Jordan. Nia. Let's go."

"Awww, Ma," Jordan whined as he navigated the PlayStation. "I'm just about to make it to the next level."

"This is not open for discussion! Let's go. *Now!*"

The fury in her voice came through loud and clear. Neither of them said another word as they grabbed their shoes and scrambled up off the floor.

Rachel made her way back down the hall and into the kitchen. "Lester, we're leaving."

Lester stood up. "Sweetie, why? What's wrong?"

"We're leaving. With or without you." Rachel snatched the keys off the table and headed to the front door. Lester took off after her.

"Rachel, wait! What's wrong?"

"See how unreasonable she is, Lester," Naomi said, following them out. "Let her go. You stay here and eat. Lord knows she ain't got nothing fixed for you at home. And on a Sunday at that."

Rachel stopped in her tracks. It took everything in her power not to go clean off on this woman. The only thing stopping her was the fact that Naomi was almost seventy-five years old and her mother had always taught her to respect the elderly.

She took a deep breath and continued outside to the car. She opened the back door and let the kids in.

"Unequally yoked, that's what you are." Naomi wagged her finger.

Rachel glared at her.

"What?" Naomi snapped. "I ain't saying nothing that ain't the truth."

Lester spun around and yelled, "Stop it, Grandma! Right now!" He stepped toward her. "I am sick and tired of you disrespecting my wife!"

Shocked that he was yelling at her, Naomi stood on her front porch, clutching her chest. "Lester!"

"You have gotten evil in your old age and I have continued to make excuses for you. Well, enough is enough! Until you accept my wife and treat her with respect, don't expect us to set foot in this house ever again."

Lester marched over, took the keys from Rachel, and climbed in the car. Rachel knew she probably should leave well enough alone, but before she climbed in the car, she couldn't help but smile and say, "Hee-haw, Mrs. Naomi, hee-haw."

chapter 30

It had been less than a week since the judge granted Jonathan visitation, but it seemed like a month. Jonathan was extremely nervous as he stood outside Angela's door. He looked at all the cars in Angela's driveway and thought maybe he should have let Rachel and David come with him to pick up Chase. Not that they could've done anything against Angela's crazy family, but he would've loved the support right about now.

Jonathan reached over and rang the doorbell. It seemed like an eternity before someone answered, even though Jonathan could clearly hear voices inside.

Finally, the door swung open. Jonathan's plastered-on smile faded when he saw Buster, Angela's ex-convict cousin.

He stood in the doorway glaring at Jonathan. "Angela, the fairy is here!" he called out, without removing his gaze or trying to disguise the look of utter contempt on his face.

Jonathan ignored his comment as he walked inside. A teary-eyed Angela stood in the entrance to the living room, tightly squeezing Chase's hand. Her parents, brother, and some other people he didn't recognize were all standing around glaring at him like they wanted to kill him dead right there. Jonathan didn't know if he should speak to them or what. He finally decided to just focus on why he'd come.

"Hi, Chase," he said, easing toward the little boy. "Do you know who I am?"

Chase slowly nodded. "My mommy said you're my daddy."

Jonathan smiled widely. "I am." His heart warmed at the sight of his mirror image.

"My mommy said you couldn't find us," Chase announced.

Jonathan looked up at Angela. He had been wondering what she was going to say to the boy. She stared at him blankly. He could sense her hatred for him.

"But I've found you now," Jonathan said, turning his attention back to Chase. "And I don't ever intend on letting you go again."

"Hmphh," Mrs. Brooks grumbled, as she stood tapping her foot. Hostility was written all over her face.

Buster stepped toward Jonathan. His broad shoulders were eye level to Jonathan. Between his size and the sixty tattoos covering his body, he definitely looked scary. "Don't let me hear about you having no punks around my lil' man here."

Jonathan wanted to tell him to go check in with his parole officer or something, but he didn't need any more drama.

"He can't do dairy products," Angela finally said.

"It makes me break out in hives," Chase proclaimed.

Jonathan studied his son. What else didn't he know about Chase? He had so much lost time to make up for.

His thoughts were interrupted by the sound of Mrs. Brooks suddenly lashing out. "How can everyone just stand around here like this is all right!"

Angela turned toward her mother. "Mother, we've been through this a thousand times. We don't have a choice." Her voice was shaking.

Mr. Brooks put his arm around his wife, obviously trying to calm her down. She jerked away.

"No! This is ridiculous. Chase doesn't know him! I can't stand you!" she screamed at Jonathan as she stepped closer to him. "I wish you were dead. I wish Angela had never met you!" Angela's brother, Darryl, grabbed Mrs. Brooks and pulled her into the kitchen as she continued to go off.

Jonathan was ready to get out of there. Chase was standing wide-eyed, obviously shaken up by his grandmother's outburst.

"Well, Chase," Jonathan said, reaching his hand to the little boy. "I have a full day planned for us. Do you like baseball?"

"Yeah, I guess so." He looked nervously toward the kitchen.

"Well, I figured we'd go check out a Houston Astros game. Then maybe go to Incredible Pizza. Does that sound like a plan?"

Chase slowly nodded. Jonathan couldn't tell if he was upset

about going with him or about the scene that had just un-
folded.

Angela lifted Chase's chin. "Baby, don't worry about
Granny. She'll be fine. She's just a little upset."

"Why doesn't she like my daddy?" Chase asked softly.

Angela hugged her son. "You know how your granny gets
worked up about stuff."

"So she's not gon' be mad at me for goin' with my daddy?"
Chase asked.

"Of course not," Angela replied. Jonathan admired how
strong she was trying to be because he could tell this was
killing her.

She pushed him toward the door. "Now, you go have fun so
you can tell me all about it, okay?"

"Okay," Chase said, finally seeming to relax. He turned to
Jonathan. "I'm ready."

Jonathan grinned as he took his son's hand and led him
outside. Chase stopped right before he got in the car and
looked up at him. "Mr. Jonathan?"

"Yes?"

"Can I call you Daddy?"

Jonathan had to swallow to get rid of the lump in his
throat. "Nothing would make me happier."

Chase flashed a huge grin as he climbed in the car. Jonathan
couldn't help but feel this was the happiest day of his life.

chapter 31

Rachel was seated next to Lester, who was at the head table looking down at his agenda. "Okay, the next order of business is what to do about the decline in tithes," Lester said as he looked over the paper in front of him.

Deacon George Wright, one of her father's friends before he tried to vote him out, passed a piece of paper to Deacon Todd Smithers, who was sitting next to him. Deacon Smithers read it, then shrugged at Deacon Wright. Like Rachel, Lester noticed the exchange.

"Gentlemen, is there a problem?" Lester asked.

Both men looked at each other. Deacon Smithers finally spoke. "Well, Reverend, some people are wondering why Sister Rachel is attending this meeting."

Rachel narrowed her eyes at the men. "Excuse me?"

"Well, I'm just saying this is church business and all," Deacon Wright chimed in.

"And I'm not a part of this church?"

"Yes, but . . ."

"Then what's the problem?" Rachel said, cocking her head.

"Well," Deacon Wright said. "We just think you need to leave the church business to the menfolk."

Rachel looked at them like they'd lost their minds. "You're kidding me, right?" When they didn't respond, she turned to Lester. He wouldn't meet her gaze. It was obvious this wasn't the first time he was hearing this protest.

"I'm always in the business meeting," she pointed out. "Why is it a problem all of a sudden?"

"Well, the board feels you're trying to change long-standing traditions by implementing all of this newfangled stuff. And we feel Zion Hill might be better served if you directed your talents somewhere else," Deacon Wright said as he fidgeted in his seat.

"Its bad enough y'all tried to run my daddy off," Rachel said, recalling the close vote to fire her father seven years ago. "He didn't go quietly and neither will I. As long as I'm first lady, I will sit in on any meeting I please."

Everyone seemed to be looking to Lester to jump in, but he just stared down at his agenda.

"Reverend Adams," Deacon Wright snapped.

Lester sighed. "We have a full agenda. Can we just get down to the next order of business?" He paused. "Brother Gipson, you have a status report on the budget?"

Brother Gipson began sifting through some papers. "Yes, according to today's offering of $12,090, we are still short of the estimated monies needed for the building fund." He looked up and shook his head. "Pastor, maybe you'd better preach on the importance of tithing next Sunday."

"I agree and I also make a motion that we send letters out to the nonpaying people suggesting that they ought to begin giving," Deacon Bishop Long said.

"I second that. I want to add an amendment that the members who tithe the most will have their names listed on the back of the church bulletin," Deacon Wright added. "And Brother Long had a great idea we were talking about earlier. On Sundays, why don't we put a microphone by the tithing basket and as members come up they can say how much they're giving. It'll be kind of an accolade for the big donors and inspire others to give just as much."

"Shoot, maybe they'll try to outdo each other." Deacon Smithers laughed.

Rachel didn't think the men could possibly be serious. She glanced around the table. Lester and another deacon looked a little uncomfortable but everyone else nodded like they thought that was the best idea they'd ever heard.

"So you mean to tell me y'all want to call out the members who aren't paying their tithes?" she asked.

She heard several groans. Deacon Wright leaned over and mumbled something to Deacon Long.

"You got something to say, Deacon?" Rachel said.

Deacon Wright sat up. "I was just saying, this is exactly why we don't want you in here, always fighting us. We know what's best for this church." Obviously frustrated, his gray eyebrows were furrowed into a V at the bridge of his nose.

"And what's best is calling folks out based on how much they're paying?" Rachel's tone was incredulous. "Maybe our members can't give their ten percent in money and spend the week giving their time to the church instead. How are you going to measure that?"

"This isn't something we came up with," Deacon Long said. "The Bible clearly states that the Lord gets His ten percent first. First fruits, remember. All that other stuff is irrelevant."

Lester rubbed his neck like he knew things were about to get ugly.

"Reverend Adams, I don't mean no disrespect, but you need to get your woman under control and let her know the menfolk got this covered," Deacon Wright growled.

Before Lester could reply, Rachel leaned forward. "Get me under control? You should know, Deacon, no one controls me. Now, if I got something on my mind, I'm gonna say it."

"Boy, ain't that the truth," someone mumbled.

Lester decided it was time he stepped in. "Look, why don't we just talk about this reasonably? We have to address the tithing issue, but maybe calling out members is not the answer."

"Then what *is* the answer?" Deacon Wright scowled. "We need to get a better infusion of funds into our coffers."

"Why? Are you in need of a new Cadillac, Deacon?" Rachel

didn't give him time to answer before turning back to the board. "Will someone please tell me where in the Bible it says you have to acknowledge what you're giving in order to honor God and edify his Kingdom?"

"I didn't even know you knew what 'edify' meant," Deacon Wright muttered.

Rachel ignored him and turned to Lester. "Lester, I think it's ridiculous to even consider this. We know half our members are struggling just to stay afloat. Our charity fund is depleted. We go start calling people out, we're sure to run them off. Yes, we want people to give their ten percent, but getting to that point is a spiritual journey our members must make on their own."

Everyone in the room frowned, except Lester. A small smile formed on his lips. He had never looked more proud.

"Rachel has a point," Lester said. "Our focus is not on forcing people to give, but helping them to grow spiritually so that they'll *want* to give."

Deacon Wright threw his pen on the table in frustration. Lester ignored him. "Let's move on to the next item on the agenda."

As Deacon Long began talking about the Men's Day program, Lester squeezed Rachel's leg under the table as he flashed her a smile. She knew exactly what he was thinking because she felt it, too. For the first time since Lester had taken over at Zion Hill, they felt like a team.

chapter 32

Rachel glanced at her watch. It was a quarter after six. She still had time to run into Walgreen's and pick up the pictures of the Good Girlz community service project before heading to their next meeting.

Rachel was so thrilled with the direction the girls were going. Even more surprising, she was amazed at the joy she was getting out of heading up the group. She really enjoyed her time with them. There were only four—two had dropped out—but she still felt like she was making a difference in their lives. She couldn't wait until Nia was old enough to join. Even though the group was mainly for troubled girls, she knew Nia would enjoy being a part of it.

Between thoughts of the group and how well she and Lester were getting along, she was in a really good mood.

Rachel pulled her car into the Walgreen's parking lot. The pictures were supposed to be ready by noon, so hopefully, she could just run in and out.

"Hello," a perky blonde said as soon as Rachel reached the counter. "How may I help you?"

"I'm here to pick up some pictures."

"Sure. One hour?"

"No, two-day processing; they're supposed to be back today."

"Okay, do you have your ticket?"

Rachel patted her jacket pocket. "Shoot. I left the ticket in the jacket I had on when I dropped the film off. It should be under Adams, first name Rachel."

"Hold on, let me check for you." The clerk looked through the stack of pictures. "I don't see . . . wait, is this it? Mrs. Lester Adams?"

"That's me." Rachel nodded. She didn't remember putting them in under that name, but oh, well.

The clerk pulled out the envelope and handed them to Rachel. "I just need you to sign this since you don't have the ticket, okay?"

"No problem." Rachel handed the woman her debit card, then scrawled her name in a thick book as the woman quickly rang her up. In less than five minutes she was back in her car. Rachel tossed the pictures on the passenger seat and made her way to the church.

Once she parked, she grabbed her purse, the pictures, and her Bible and looked around. "Good, I beat everyone here,"

Rachel mumbled. The last thing she wanted was for the girls to be waiting outside the church.

Rachel unlocked the door and went into her office. She put her belongings on her desk and smiled as she picked up the pictures. She was so proud of how well their community service project had gone. Rachel opened the envelope and pulled out the pictures. The smile left her face as she looked at the first picture: a tall white woman holding a Pekingese puppy, a huge smile across her face. *Why does that woman look familiar?* Rachel flipped to the next picture, which showed the woman in a sexy negligee. Then, suddenly, it dawned on Rachel: "It's that floozy from church!" she exclaimed. "How did her pictures get mixed up with mine?"

Rachel flipped through the pictures, each one showing the woman in a different provocative pose, wearing less and less clothing. Rachel was about to throw the photos in the trash when she came across the last batch of pictures. The first was a photo of Lester sitting in someone's dining room, the woman on his lap. They both had huge smiles on their faces. Rachel's mouth dropped open in stunned disbelief. The next picture was of the woman as she leaned in and kissed Lester; the last was of the woman, Lester, and the dog. They looked like one big happy family.

Rachel felt like she was going to be sick. *What was Lester doing with this woman? Why did she look so blissfully in love?* Her head began pounding and her vision became blurry. "There's got to be an explanation. I'm not seeing what I think I'm seeing," she mumbled, squeezing the pictures in her hand.

A knock on the door made her jump. She quickly stuffed the crumpled pictures into her purse. "Yes," she said, trying to make sure her voice didn't crack.

"It's Camille and Angel."

Rachel had to make herself calm down. The Good Girlz group was here and she needed to put the pictures out of her mind.

"Ummm, I'm coming." She took a minute to compose herself before standing and making her way to the door. "Hi, girls," she said as she swung the door open.

"Hi, Miss Rachel," said Camille, the leader of the group. "We were just wondering if we could bail on tonight's meeting. It's the big game tonight, Madison against Yates."

"Yeah," Angel chimed in. "We forgot to ask about it. I know Jasmine isn't going to be here because her brother is playing."

"And we've already talked to Alexis, she's just down the street, but she wants to go to the game, too. Please, please, please," Camille begged.

If only they knew! Their pleas were music to Rachel's ears. "Okay, fine. You girls go have fun and I'll see you next week."

Both girls looked like they were surprised to get a yes from Rachel so quickly. They hugged her before taking off.

Rachel plopped back down in the chair. She was tempted to go find Lester and just start beating the hell out of him, but she had to think this through. For once in her life she had to be sensible. She couldn't just go off half-cocked thinking about how she was going to kill Lester. She had to carefully plan how she was going to kill him.

Rachel took the pictures out of her purse. Her chest felt tight, squeezing her heart painfully. She contemplated calling her husband's cell phone. No, she didn't need to talk to him. Not yet. There was no explaining it. Pictures didn't lie. No wonder he'd been so quick to want to forgive that floozy! He was the one she was having an affair with. And the woman had come into church probably to taunt Lester. Or maybe just to mess with her. How could he do this to her? *Why* would he do this to her? This tramp was so brazen that she'd even put her pictures under *Mrs.* Lester Adams. Did she *want* Rachel to find them? Or was that how she actually saw herself?

Rachel had so many questions and so few answers. *But you'd better believe I'm going to get some answers.*

She stood up, took a deep breath, and prepared herself to head home, shaking her head as she willed the tears back. "Lester Lawrence Adams, there had better be an explanation for this. Because if not, you picked the wrong woman to cheat on," she said as she closed the door to her office and headed home.

chapter 33

Rachel eased the front door open. The light was on in the study, which meant Lester was still hard at work on his sermon. She was trying to be quiet, but Lester must have heard her and came into the hall.

"Hey, honey. I was worried. I've been calling your cell phone. Where have you been? It's almost midnight."

Rachel looked at him, but didn't say anything. She wanted to scratch his eyes out. But she had to deal with this like a mature, reasonable adult. She had been driving around for hours in a daze, her cell phone turned off, trying to get her head together before she came home. She'd thought about calling Sister Morgan, but truthfully, she wasn't in a praying mood right now. The only prayer she had been able to form was, "Lord, please don't let me kill my husband."

"So, what, you're not going to answer me?" Lester asked. "Have you been out at the club again? I've told you before, that is not befitting of a preacher's wife."

Rachel slowly walked toward him, her voice steady as she spoke. "You know, Reverend Adams, what *is* befitting of a preacher's wife? Should she be forgiving?"

Lester looked bewildered. "What are you talking about?"

Rachel leaned against the wall and crossed her arms. It was taking everything in her power to stay calm. "Should she be understanding? Should she be a fool?"

"Rachel, will you please tell me what you are talking about?"

"Tell me, Reverend, have you heard back from the floozy who stood up and confessed her affair at church?"

"What? Why are we talking about her again?"

Rachel could've sworn she saw a hint of nervousness cross his face. She threw her hands up as she sauntered into the study and over to his desk. She picked up a photo of her and Lester taken in Jamaica last year. "Oh, I don't know. I was thinking, I wonder if the man she was having an affair with felt bothered at all by her testimony," she said as she fingered the picture.

"I . . . I'm sure."

"Are you?" Rachel placed the picture facedown. "Tell me something, do you think it's hypocritical to get up in the pulpit Sunday morning and talk about walking a path of righteousness and yet be the biggest whore in the church?"

"Rachel, where are you going with this?"

Rachel walked around and stood right in front of Lester.

"Tell me, Reverend, had you counseled the adulteress prior to her coming into the church?"

"What? I—I told you I didn't know her."

Rachel studied his face. He had started to sweat. She walked away, trying to calm herself again, but she could no longer hold it in. "Liar!" she screamed. "You no-good, hypocritical, lying dog!" She picked up the cordless telephone and threw it at Lester's head. He ducked and the phone smashed into the wall.

"Rachel, what is your problem?" Lester yelled.

"You want to know my problem?" Rachel shouted. She reached into her purse and grabbed the pictures. "*You* are my problem. You and your lying mistress!" She threw the pictures at him.

Lester stared at her, then slowly bent to pick up the photos. "Oh, my God," he muttered when he saw them.

"Don't call on God now, you—"

"Baby, I can explain," he said, stepping toward her.

Rachel held her hands up and backed away. "There is nothing to explain and nothing for you to say, except that you will be out of this house in the next hour."

"Rachel, you've got to be kidding me. It's after midnight."

"Do I look like I care what time it is? Get out, Lester." Rachel nodded as she silently counted backward from ten. She was doing good. If he just left now, there wouldn't be any real drama.

Lester tried to pull her into his arms. So much for staying calm. Rachel felt herself losing it. "I said get out!" She hit him in the chest. "You lying, stinking, dirty, hypocrite. Get out!"

Lester put his hands up to shield himself from her blows.

"I trusted you! You were a pimply faced boy when I met you! I brought you out of your shell. I gave you my heart and this is how you repay me!" Rachel couldn't help it, the tears had now started coming. "You stand up there every morning and preach about love, trust, and following God's word. How dare you?"

Lester looked like he wanted to cry, too. "Rachel, I'm s . . . I'm sorry. I never meant to hurt you."

Rachel swung at him again. "So you admit it, you lying bastard?"

Lester plopped down on the sofa and buried his face in his hands. "I never meant for this to happen."

"What? You never meant for what to happen? Getting caught?" Rachel's chest heaved up and down as she sobbed uncontrollably.

"No, I mean, I never meant to get caught up with Mary."

Rachel viciously wiped away her tears as she struggled to compose herself. She was surprised she hadn't awakened the kids but their rooms were on the other side of the house, not to mention they were both sound sleepers. "That's right. Her name is Mary. Like the Virgin Mary. What a joke. She stood up in that church and made a mockery of God. Of me. Of you." She laughed, but it came out sounding like a cry of pain.

Lester kept his face buried.

Rachel screamed, "How long has this been going on? How long have you been making a fool out of me?"

"It was only a few months. But it's over."

"A few? As in two, four, twelve, what?"

"About three months. But I stopped seeing her two months ago."

"Does everyone at the church know?"

Lester lifted his head, tears filling his eyes. "No one knows."

Rachel took a deep breath as she willed back the tears. How could she have been so blind? "Three months. Did you two have a good laugh when she got up at church?"

"No, no," Lester said desperately. "She came to the church because I wouldn't take her calls or agree to see her anymore."

"Where did you meet her?"

Lester tried to reach out to Rachel. "Maybe you should sit down."

"I don't want to sit down. I want you to answer the question!"

"I met Mary when I was visiting another church. I never meant to get involved with her, but . . . she just kept telling me how wonderful I am. She . . . she made me feel like a man—something you never do," he quietly added.

"Oh, so now this is *my* fault?" Rachel screamed. He definitely wasn't making things better.

"No, that's not what I'm saying. I just . . ."

"No, what you need to be saying is that you cheated because you *wanted* to cheat."

Lester sighed; he knew this was an argument he couldn't win.

"Do you love her?" Rachel didn't know if she was ready to know the answer to that question, but she had to ask.

"Of course not," Lester replied, a pleading look in his eyes. "I only slept with her a couple of times."

"Oh, is that all? That makes it okay, then," Rachel snapped sarcastically. It felt like someone had taken a knife and was twisting it in her heart.

"I swear. I just . . . I was just more emotionally involved with her than anything else. I just made a mistake. A horrible, horrible mistake."

Rachel closed her eyes and tried once again to compose herself. "When's the last time you saw her?"

"Right after church that day she came in. I met her later to ask her why she'd done that."

Rachel snapped her eyes open to stare at Lester, waiting for him to go on. "And?"

"And she said she was trying to send a message to me that she wouldn't go away easily. Rachel, I only got involved with her in the first place because . . . because she made me feel really good about myself."

"I bet she did." Rachel turned her back to her husband and struggled to stop the tears.

"Baby, I'm trying to be honest," Lester said.

Rachel spun around. "Honesty? Oh, you mean you actually know what that is?"

Lester sighed. "I just went to her because she was constantly telling me how I deserved to be treated and that she could do that."

"That's a cop-out, Lester!"

"Maybe, but it's the truth. The thing is, I realized I had

made a mistake. I didn't want to lose you. I didn't want to hurt you. I begged God to forgive me and I ended it with her. At least, I tried to end it. She wouldn't let me leave, saying she was in love and deserved to be with me. She kept threatening to do something, but I never thought she'd actually show up at the church."

Rachel stared at him through tear-filled eyes. Never in a million years did she think she'd be at this place in her life. She never thought *Lester*, of all people, would do this to her. Rachel closed her eyes, willing the tears to stop. She smiled before opening her eyes and staring at her husband.

"Exodus 20:14."

Lester lowered his head.

"What does the Word say, because you must not have read it?" Rachel asked, her voice laced with authority.

"'Thou shall not commit adultery.'"

Rachel headed to the door, but stopped and turned around. "Romans 12:19."

Lester stared up at his wife, confused. "'Vengeance is mine saith the Lord'?"

"Just so you know, I'm not gon' wait on the Lord." She walked out of the study. "I'm going to sleep in the guest room. I want you gone when I wake up or you will really and truly know vengeance." Rachel didn't give him a chance to respond as she made her way upstairs.

chapter 34

Every fiber of her being was telling Rachel to turn around and take her butt home. She'd driven around for almost two hours after awaking to find Lester gone. He'd left some funky note, reiterating how sorry he was and telling her he would give her time to cool off but that he wasn't giving up on her.

He might as well give up on her. Because she was as good as gone. And her being here proved it.

Rachel fought off the tears that were trying to make their way down her cheeks. She had been a good and faithful wife. Sure, she'd been difficult at times, had even been tempted by Bobby a couple of times, but she'd never crossed that line. *Do not cry. Do not cry.* She repeated the mantra over and over in her head as she stood on the porch of the ranch-style home.

After a few more deep breaths, Rachel pressed the doorbell. Nope, she'd never crossed the line. But that was about to change.

The door swung open. Bobby gazed at her in confusion. "Rachel?" He stuck his head out of the door and looked around. "I didn't know you were coming by." He stepped aside and motioned for her to come in. "Where's Jordan?"

Rachel walked past him and stepped inside. "He's with my brother."

"What's going on?" Bobby asked as he closed the door. "Is something wrong with Jordan?"

Rachel threw her purse down on the sofa and inhaled deeply. *An eye for an eye.* She turned to Bobby and forced a smile. "Nothing is wrong. Can't I just stop by to say hello to the father of my child?"

He looked at her suspiciously. "You want to tell me what's really going on?"

She stepped in front of Bobby, so close she could feel his breath. "I just wanted to see you, maybe talk for a little while. That's all," she softly said. "But if you want me to go, I'll go."

Bobby looked like he still wasn't convinced. Rachel licked her lips and shot him an innocent look. "Hey, you got anything to drink around here? Like wine?" she asked. Yeah, it wasn't even two in the afternoon, but she had to loosen up. She was about to take a step back and kill all the progress she'd made over these years. But it was Lester's fault. As bad as she wanted Bobby, she would've never acted on it. At least not before she'd seen those pictures.

"Yeah, I got some wine in there. But should you be drinking? You know, because of your position in the church and all?"

Rachel looked around the room. "I don't see any deacons now, do you? Besides, I told y'all, I'm no ordinary first lady." She watched Bobby walk into the kitchen. "And I won't be a first lady for long either," she muttered.

"What did you say?" he asked, turning back toward her.

"Nothing. Just come on back with the wine." Rachel sat on the sofa and leaned back, trying her best to get any feelings of guilt out of her mind. She couldn't believe she was feeling torn. She needed to show Lester he didn't know who he was messing with.

Bobby returned with two glasses of white zinfandel. He handed Rachel a glass. She took it, a seductive smile across her face. "So, are you and Shante really over?"

"As over as they come."

"So what did you do?" Rachel asked.

Bobby laughed. "Why is it me who had to do anything? Nope, Shante wanted kids. I didn't. She wanted Charmin. I wanted Angel Soft. We just fought all the time, about any and everything. Then she had her people all up in our business all the time. Just call it irreconcilable differences."

Rachel nodded. She recalled how heartbroken she'd been when they'd gotten married. Bobby must've been thinking about the same thing because he said, "You know, when you showed up at my wedding, what did you hope to accomplish?"

Rachel looked away. She couldn't believe she had been so stupid. That day was so embarrassing. She'd actually gotten into a fight with Shante after trying to kiss Bobby. She'd been hoping to break up the wedding, but they got married anyway. "I don't know. I guess I just wanted to convince you that you shouldn't marry her."

Bobby raised Rachel's chin and looked her in the eyes. "I wish I had listened."

"I wish I'd done a lot of things differently, Bobby."

They sat staring at each other in silence for a few minutes before Bobby leaned in. Rachel's heart started beating fast. He gently touched his lips to hers. She closed her eyes. *What am I doing?* She felt her body growing weak. Bobby pulled her to him and kissed her harder. Rachel let herself sink into his embrace. She had dreamed about this day since they broke up nine years ago—but it wasn't making her feel like she always thought it would.

Bobby eased her down on the sofa, then gently ran his hand up her leg. "Rachel, I have never stopped loving you," he whispered.

Rachel tried to speak, but no words would come out. She squeezed her eyes tightly. It did feel good being in Bobby's arms. *What are you doing?* There went that little voice again. Suddenly Rachel saw images of her mother. She was looking on disapprovingly. *You have grown into such a strong woman. Don't let temptation wreck all that you've worked for,* her mother warned. Rachel quickly opened her eyes. Bobby had started unbuttoning her blouse. He was moaning as he nibbled her neck. *For God's sakes, you're a married woman!* the little voice screamed. *But Lester cheated on me. So? Don't let his infidelity block your blessings.* It felt like the two voices were playing Ping-Pong in her head. Rachel shook her head and pushed Bobby away. "Wait."

"Please, Rachel. You just don't know how long I've wanted you." He leaned in and tried to kiss her again.

Rachel pulled herself up. "Bobby, I . . . I can't." She started buttoning her blouse. "I can't. I'm married. It's not right."

"It's not right for two people who love each other to deny their feelings," Bobby whispered. "We've denied them for too long. You don't love him like you love me. You'll never love anyone like you love me."

Rachel stared at him. Her heart was beating so fast, she thought it would come bursting out of her chest. He was so right about that. "Regardless, I made a promise to my husband. To God."

Bobby looked agitated. "What did you come over here for then? And since when did you become a woman of your word?" He looked like he immediately regretted saying that.

Rachel glared at Bobby. She knew that came from the fact that she hadn't been faithful to him. "Since the day I said 'I do.'" She reached down and picked up her purse before heading toward the door.

Bobby grabbed her arm. "I'm sorry, I didn't mean that. It's just that I've waited so long for this. For you. I know you want me, too. I can feel it. And I know being a minister's wife doesn't excite you." He stepped in closer to her. His breath was hot, yet it sent chills up her spine.

Rachel took a deep breath. "Bobby, you may be right. But

the fact remains that I am Lester's wife. Until, or if, that changes, I can't be here with you like this. I'm so sorry for leading you on. I . . . I thought I could do this, but I can't." Rachel stepped around him and quickly made her way out the door.

She sat in her car in a daze. She couldn't believe she had walked out on Bobby. In her heart, she'd always felt like he was the man for her. Lester's infidelity had confirmed that. So why was she now so unsure?

"I don't know," she mumbled to herself. "Maybe I have to close this chapter with Lester before I can deal with Bobby." Yes, she thought as she started her car. She needed to get Lester out of her life. Then she could focus on the man she was really meant to be with.

chapter 35

Rachel watched Nia chase her mother's dog, Brandy, around the living room of her father's house. It had been just over a week since she'd put Lester out. He'd left a hundred messages saying he was at his grandmother's whenever she was ready to talk. Hmmph! As far as she was concerned, she'd never be ready.

She'd come to her father's house so Lester could go home and get some clothes—she had no desire to see him. She'd left that message for him on his cell phone, but other than that she had made no attempt to talk to him, nor did she have any desire to.

"So, are you just gon' skip church this morning?" Simon said as he made his way into the living room. He was holding a mug filled to the brim with black coffee.

"Yep, Zion Hill can make it a couple of Sundays without me there. It's not like they like me anyway," Rachel replied.

Simon sat down next to her. "I know this is not my daughter I hear sounding dejected."

Rachel stared at him. They had had their share of battles, and growing up, she didn't agree with half the things he did, but she had really grown to respect him over these last few years. "Daddy, can I ask you something?"

"You can ask me anything, baby."

"Did you ever cheat on Mama?"

Simon smiled. "Why did I know that was coming?"

Rachel shrugged. "You can tell me the truth."

"Yeah, sure, tell my daughter about my infidelities." He chuckled.

Rachel's eyes grew wide. "So you were unfaithful?"

Simon grinned. "No, sweetheart. I never cheated on your mother. I came close one time, but your mother called and told me she was pregnant with David and I took that as a sign. I'm not gon' lie, there was a lot of temptation."

"Yeah, like Delilah," Rachel said, recalling her father's church secretary, who let it be known how much she wanted Rev. Simon Jackson.

Simon laughed. "No, as much as Delilah threw herself at me, I was never tempted by her. Everyone else may not have thought your mother was all that, but to me she was the most beautiful woman on the planet. But I am still a man, and there were some worldly women who didn't hesitate to use their worldly goods to try and tempt me to do wrong. I called them the devil's workers."

"Well, why didn't you ever give in to temptation?"

"Honestly, as much as I'd like to say I was trying to honor God, I was really honoring your mother. She gave me everything I ever wanted or needed. I had to ask myself, why go anywhere else when I got everything I need at home." Simon narrowed his eyes at her. "Did Lester have everything he needed at home? Just something to think about." He squeezed Rachel's hand.

Rachel looked at her father in surprise. "How did you know?"

"Now you know that boy called me before he got out the door."

"I suppose you're going to take his side, tell me how I should have been a better wife."

"On the contrary. He's responsible for his own actions. He's a grown man. But I do want you to ask yourself—were you a good wife?"

"I think I was."

Simon looked at her and smiled. "If you think so, then that's all that matters." Simon patted her leg as he stood up. "Me myself, I'm feeling good today for a change. Brenda is on her way to take me to church."

Rachel cut her eyes. She still wasn't feeling this relationship her father had with Brenda Bailey, but right now, she had bigger things to worry about.

Simon headed to the door. "I'm going to wait on the porch. But Rachel," he said, turning to her.

"Yes, Daddy?"

"I don't condone nothing he did, but I know that boy. He is truly sorry. Have you thought about forgiving him?"

Rachel looked at her father like he was crazy. "Yeah, right. Once a dog, always a dog in my book."

Simon nodded. "I know you've never made any mistakes in your life that would need to be forgiven, but it happens."

Rachel narrowed her eyes. "You're trying to be funny, huh?"

"I'm just saying everybody needs forgiveness at some time or another. I'm saying pray on it. Think about that. I'm not saying you need to stay with him. But ask God to guide your decision. He won't steer you wrong." Simon turned and walked out the door.

Hmphh, Rachel thought. She may not have been as assimilated in the Word as her father and Lester, but she was sure about one thing—no way would God want her with a man who cheated on her.

chapter 36

Rachel watched her husband in the pulpit. He seemed to be reaching deep in his soul to bring the word of God to the congregation. Too bad he didn't listen to his own message about being faithful to God's Word.

Rachel had on her smiling first lady face today. But in actuality, she wanted to claw Lester's eyes out. He'd chosen something safe to preach about, something about thanking God for the little things. Rachel didn't really know because her mind was too clouded with hate at the moment. She kept looking at him, imagining him with that woman.

She'd only come to church because her Good Girlz group was being honored at today's service. Otherwise, she would've stayed at home, even though it would have been her third Sunday in a row missing church, and people were sure to start talking. Not that she cared what anyone thought, anyway. She had been getting funny stares from people all throughout service, no doubt wondering where she'd been. It was obvious no one knew she and Lester were having problems because she definitely would've heard the gossip by now. That was what Rachel hated most about some so-called Christians: they were the biggest gossipers and rumormongers around.

For a brief moment, Rachel wished she had canceled today's presentation. She quickly shook that thought off. The Good Girlz program was being honored by the mayor's office for outstanding community service for all the work they'd been doing with the senior citizens' centers. The girls were extremely excited; truth be told, she was quite proud herself.

Lester had seemed genuinely excited to see her when she'd walked into the church office this morning. He'd asked her if she was going to give the welcome, which Sister Ida Hicks had been giving in her absence. Rachel responded with a glare and went on into her office without answering him. She knew having Ida welcome the guests with her sitting in the congregation was only fueling the rumor fires; again, she just couldn't make herself care.

Rachel did manage to put her anger out of her mind when the mayor's assistant took the podium and presented the award to the girls. Rachel beamed with pride as Camille stepped to the microphone.

"We just want to thank the first lady, and our second mother, Mrs. Rachel Adams, for believing in us, pushing us, bringing us together, and creating this program, which not only helps others, but has helped all of us in turning our lives around," Camille said.

Tears filled Rachel's eyes as she walked to the front and hugged the girls. The congregation was on their feet applauding. Rachel couldn't help but smile, especially because so many people had been against her starting this group. If anyone questioned whether she was making a difference in this church, this should be enough to show them that she was.

After the service, Rachel said good-bye to the Good Girlz—Alexis, Camille, Jasmine, and Angel. She tried to make her exit quickly, but Ida and Birdie Mae and her cohorts were lying in wait.

"Hello, Sister Adams," Ida said. "What a nice honor."

Rachel feigned a smile. "Thank you." Ida had been one of the main ones against her starting the Good Girlz.

"We sho' been missing you in church," Ida replied.

Rachel stared at the old biddies. Like they really missed her. "Thank you for your concern." She could tell they were fishing for more.

"Yep, two Sundays in a row. Have you been sick?" Birdie Mae said.

Yeah, sick of y'all hypocrites and your lying pastor, she wanted to say. "No, ma'am. I'm just fine. Well, I have to run. You all have a blessed day." Rachel walked away before anyone could bombard her with more questions.

She made her way into the office where she spent the next twenty minutes checking her messages, which she hadn't done all week. Most of the phone calls were from people who were interested in the Good Girlz, including a newspaper reporter who wanted to do an article on them. That brought a smile to Rachel's face. The girls would love that.

Rachel saw the button on Lester's phone light up, which meant he was in his office. She quickly gathered her things. She still wasn't ready to talk to him, her pain and anger were too deep.

She blew out a frustrated breath. Unfortunately, she had to pass by his office to leave. Hopefully, he would be engrossed on the phone and she could sneak by. Of course, just when she tiptoed past him, he looked up and called out to her.

"Rachel, please. Can we talk just for a minute?" He rose.

Rachel stopped and folded her arms. "Fine, let's hear what lie you have to tell today." She walked into his office and sat down in a chair in front of his desk. She knew it wasn't helping anything for her to be so mean, but she just couldn't seem to get rid of the anger that was filling her heart.

Instead of taking his seat back behind the desk, he sat down next to her. He looked weary, like he'd aged ten years in the last four weeks. "Rachel, I cannot begin to tell you how sorry I am."

"You said that already," she snapped, rolling her eyes to the ceiling.

Lester sighed. "And I can't say it enough. I don't know what I was thinking. I'm not saying this to make excuses because I am totally responsible for my actions, but it just felt good to have someone . . . I don't know . . . someone take an interest in me." He leaned back in the chair. "By no means am I laying blame on you, but when's the last time you told me I was handsome, or that you were proud of me? When's the last time you even took my feelings into account? I guess being with Mary just made me feel like a man for a change. I know I wasn't your first choice for a husband. I know that had Bobby even remotely given you the time of day, I would've been history." He fought back tears. "I've never had your heart. I thought I could love you into loving me. But it never happened. You settled when you married me and I feel it every day."

Rachel felt tears forming as well. She knew she had never been lovey-dovey with Lester, but she did love him. Not on the same level as the love she'd once had for Bobby, but do you ever really recapture your first love?

Lester continued. "Again, please don't think I'm laying blame at your feet. I just want you to know what drove me to do what I did. I know it was my own weakness that is responsible for the pain you—that we both—are in. And all I'm saying is that if you will give me another chance, if you will allow me back into that little corner of your heart that you had given me, I promise I'll never let you down again."

Rachel stared him. She could see the sincerity all over his face. "Are you still seeing her?" she asked softly.

"No. I stopped seeing her before she came to the church that day."

Rachel was conflicted. Why wasn't she cursing him out? Why wasn't she going off on him?

"I'm asking, no, I'm begging you for another chance," Lester pleaded.

Rachel took a deep breath. She was so confused. She shouldn't even be talking to him.

"Please, Rachel. I will devote my life to making this up to you. We can go to counseling, anything. Just don't throw us away."

Rachel looked away. She didn't want him to see the tears that had started trickling down her cheeks. "Lester, I can't make you any promises. But I'm open to counseling."

Lester's eyes lit up. "Oh, baby, thank you. I'll call Reverend Cassidy at New Pilgrim. He's a counselor—"

"Unh-unh." Rachel cut him off. "If I do this, I want to go to a professional. I don't need any of your preacher friends telling me how God intended for us to stick together for better or for worse. I'm not in that place right now. Right now, I want to deal with getting to the root of our problems. I'll keep praying but right now, we need professional counseling."

"That's fine, baby. Whatever you want. I'll find a professional tomorrow." Lester reached over and squeezed her hand. "You won't regret this."

Rachel's gaze met her husband's. She still couldn't believe she was even allowing him into her space. What had gotten into her to even consider giving him another chance? "I hope not, because . . ." Her voice trailed off as she glanced over her shoulder and toward the door of Lester's office. Mary stood there with a surprised look on her face, like she definitely wasn't expecting to see Rachel there. Rachel slowly stood as her chest began to heave up and down.

"Oh, I'm sorry. I didn't mean to interrupt," Mary said. "I'll come back later." She quickly turned to leave.

"No, wait," Rachel called out. Mary stopped and turned around. Rachel glared at her husband; any sympathy she'd felt for him was gone now. She turned her attention back toward the woman. "You have a lot of nerve showing your face around here."

"You didn't tell me she'd be here," Mary hissed to Lester.

"What?" Rachel was about to lose it for sure now. "What is she talking about, Lester? You knew she was coming?"

"He invited me." Mary seemed to have gained some new-found confidence.

Oh, it was about to be on for real! "You invited her? You sit here and feed me all this bull about making our marriage work and your mistress was headed here?"

Lester stood, vigorously shaking his head. "It's not what it looks like, Rachel. I did ask her here, but to plead with her to leave me alone."

Mary laughed. "You can believe that if you want to."

Rachel took two steps toward the woman. Lester grabbed her arm. "Rachel, please."

Rachel snatched her arm away. "Don't put your hands on me. Ever again."

"I told you she was not the type of woman you needed, Lester." Mary turned toward Rachel. "You have a king, sweetheart, and you don't even know it. Most black women don't. He told me how you barely make love to him, how selfish you are. Didn't your mother ever tell you what you won't do for your man, someone else will?"

That was it. Rachel lunged toward the woman and snatched

her by the hair. Mary screamed as Rachel flung her to the ground. She tried to stand up, her hair sticking up wildly all over her head. "This is what you want, Lester? Some low-class, fighting woman?" she cried, rubbing her bruised head.

"I told you I loved my wife, Mary." Lester looked like he couldn't believe this was happening.

Mary tossed her hair back. "If you loved her so much, then what were you doing with me?"

"Yeah, Lester!" Rachel said. "If you love me so much, what were you doing with her?"

Lester buried his head in his hands. "I made a terrible mistake."

"You got that right!" She snarled at Mary, "Look, you home-wrecking adulterer, you can have him. He's all yours. May you both rot in hell."

She couldn't believe she'd almost given Lester another chance. This was God's way of stopping her, that much she was sure about.

Rachel slipped her pump back on her foot and strutted off with her head held high.

chapter 37

Rachel couldn't help but smile as she watched her brother cradle D.J. in his arms. The tiny baby was finally having a rare content moment. His jitteriness had stopped and he was hungrily sucking a bottle. David stared at him as if he'd never known such joy. Rachel enjoyed being around D.J., too. When she was focused on him, she didn't have to think about Lester or her marriage. It had been a week since that fiasco at the church and Lester knew what was good for him because he hadn't been beating down her door begging for another chance.

"You're really taking to this fatherhood thing, huh?" Rachel wiggled D.J.'s toes.

"Yeah," David replied, never taking his eyes off the baby. "I finally feel like my life has purpose. I swear I'm going to give my little boy the best of everything."

Rachel loved seeing the love in her brother's eyes. He hadn't seemed so happy in years. D.J. was doing remarkably better, and Rachel had no doubt that was because of her brother's unconditional love.

David finally broke out of the trance he seemed to be in as he watched his son. He rose from the chair. "Rachel, I'm going to go lay D.J. down, then I need to talk to you about something."

"Of course. I'll be right here," Rachel said. She picked up an *Ebony* magazine, leaned back, and started flipping through the pages while she waited on David.

Five minutes later he was back downstairs and sitting beside her on the sofa. "I need your help, Rachel."

Rachel looked at her brother suspiciously. "David, I don't have any money."

David stopped her before she could go off on a tirade. "Sis, this isn't about money. I need your help in order to keep my son."

Now that Rachel could do. "You know I'll help with that. Just tell me what you need."

David rubbed his head like he was really stressed out. That peaceful look he'd had just a few minutes ago was gone. "Tawny is demanding money in exchange for D.J."

"What? That's crazy." Rachel sat up.

"Tawny *is* crazy. She wants ten thousand dollars."

"I hope you told her what she could do."

"No. I told her I would get it."

"Why in the world would you do that?"

David got up and started pacing. "I'm desperate, Rachel. If she takes my son, she'll end up selling him for a bag of rocks, or she'll just leave him with some stranger while she goes and gets high. I can't have my child on the streets. I *won't* have him on the streets. Not for one day."

"But, David, blackmail is not the answer. I mean, fight her for custody. I'm sure a judge would side with you."

"Now you sound like Jonathan. Can you promise me a judge will side with me, Rachel? Or will he say neither one of us is fit and put my child in foster care? Besides, like I told Jonathan, I don't have time for all that. Now will you help me or not?"

Rachel could tell from the determined look on David's face that he would do whatever he could to keep his son away from Tawny. "I'll help, but I don't know that giving her money is the answer. She'll just keep coming back for more."

"I know that," David said. "Which is why I think I've found a solution."

Rachel stared at her brother. David's plan had better be pretty good because Tawny was a hustler if Rachel had ever seen one. And she wasn't going to go away lightly.

"She's on her way over here. She thinks it's to collect some of the money. I need you to help me with something."

Rachel didn't want to get caught up in any drama. She had enough of her own. But this was her nephew they were talking about. "Just let me know what I need to do."

David had just finished filling Rachel in on his plan when the doorbell rang. He handed her a wad of cash. "They're already marked."

"You go check on D.J. I'll get the door," Rachel said as she dropped the money in her purse, which she set on the coffee table.

She squeezed her brother's arm as she watched him standing there, staring at the door. "This will work."

David looked at her with tears in his eyes. "I hope so." He turned and made his way upstairs while Rachel went to answer the door.

"What's up, baby girl!" Tawny sang.

Rachel's mouth dropped open at the sight of Tawny. She wore a fire-red, strapless spandex dress and platform boots. Her long blonde and red braids were covered with a black bandana. Her braless breasts were sagging and the dark circles under her eyes made her look like she hadn't slept in days.

"Hello, Tawny." Rachel stood in the entrance, looking her up and down.

Tawny peeked around her. "You gon' let me in to see my baby?"

Rachel reluctantly stepped aside. She was as determined as David now. No way would she let her nephew go with this psycho.

"Where my boo?" Tawny couldn't say two words without rubbing her arms.

"D.J. is upstairs sleeping."

"I was talking about David. Although I did bring this for the kid." She held out a dirty teddy bear, which was missing one eye.

"Ummm, okay." Rachel used her thumb and forefinger to take the teddy bear. She sat the filthy thing on the end table and turned back to Tawny, who had reached under her arm and was vigorously scratching. Rachel tried not to let her disgust show.

"David! Your baby mama is here!" Tawny shouted.

"Would you lower your voice?" Rachel said. "Your son is asleep."

"Everybody always worried about that stupid kid. What about me?"

Rachel stared at Tawny in disbelief. She contemplated saying something but decided what was the use. If anything, she'd say an extra prayer for Tawny tonight because homegirl was gone.

Rachel shook her head as David walked into the living room. Tawny's eyes lit up. "Hey, baby. You got my loot?"

David looked at Rachel. She nodded. "I'll let you all have some privacy." Rachel glanced at her purse, which was sitting on the coffee table wide open. "I'll be in the kitchen." Rachel walked into the kitchen, made a phone call, then immediately leaned against the door to eavesdrop.

"Tawny, I'm not going to have your money until tomorrow," she heard David say.

Tawny's tone immediately changed. "No you didn't. I already gave you some extra time. I was 'posed to have this money two weeks ago and you keep comin' up with all these excuses. I guess you think I'm playing! I told yo' sorry—"

"Tawny, chill," David calmly said. "I told you it wasn't going to be easy but I got it."

"You did?" she asked suspiciously.

"Yeah, but I can't pick it up until tomorrow."

"David, I ain't playing with you. I'm taking the kid if you ain't got my money tomorrow. Got me coming all the way over here. Bus fare ain't cheap."

"I'll have it tomorrow," David promised.

Rachel took that as her cue and quickly grabbed her cell phone and punched in her father's home phone number. She picked up the phone after two rings, waited a minute, then stuck her head back out in the living room. "David, telephone. I think it's that call you were waiting on," Rachel said. She actually felt funny about lying, which totally surprised her because she used to be a master liar. But she told herself what they were doing was necessary for D.J.'s sake.

"I'll be right back," David told Tawny. He walked into the kitchen. "Did you call them?" he asked Rachel.

"Yeah, they're on their way. I just hope they get here quickly."

"Cool." David nodded anxiously.

The two of them made their way around to the dining-room entrance so they could spy on Tawny.

Tawny stood, impatiently tapping her foot and rubbing her arms. It took her only a few minutes to notice Rachel's purse. She glanced around the room, waited a minute, then eased over to the purse. In one swift move, she had pulled out the wallet, removed the money and credit cards, and put the wallet back in Rachel's purse.

Both Rachel and David smiled. "How did you know it would be this easy?" Rachel whispered.

"Because I know Tawny," David replied. He glanced out the window. "And there are the cops, right on time. Come on."

David made his way back into the living room and Tawny jumped over to the pictures on the mantel, acting like she was studying them.

"A'ight, Tawny. It's all set. I'll have everything tomorrow," David said.

"That's what I'm talking 'bout," Tawny replied as she headed to the door. "And just remember, I ain't playing with you."

"Don't you want to see D.J.?" David asked, stalling for time.

"For what?" Tawny asked.

"Ummm, maybe because he's your child," Rachel offered.

Tawny laughed. "Right, right. Naw, tell him I said hi. I got a meeting to get to." Tawny swung the door open to face two uniformed policemen. David looked on in anticipation.

"What y'all want?" Tawny snapped.

The officer looked over her shoulder at David. "Is this the woman we got the call about?"

David nodded.

"What y'all talking about?" Tawny looked around uneasily. "Whatever." She threw her arms up. "Move, po-po."

"Ma'am, we'll have to ask you to empty your bag." The taller officer motioned toward the small bag she had strapped around her body.

"I ain't emptying nothing. You got a warrant?"

"Ma'am, I will ask you one more time."

"You can ask a hundred more times. I ain't emptying nothing." She pushed the officer aside and tried to go around him.

Both officers then grabbed her and forced her to the ground. Tawny was kicking, screaming, and cursing like a madwoman.

One officer managed to get her purse. He opened it and pulled out the cash. "Well, well, well."

"Three thousand dollars. All marked," David said.

Tawny glared at David with hatred. "You set me up? You piece of—"

"Hey, Raybo," the taller officer said, cutting her off. "Look what else we got." He started pulling stuff out of her purse. "A crack pipe, some weed, and what would you say this is?" He dangled a Ziploc bag.

"Looks like a hundred dollars' worth of rocks," the other officer replied as he slapped cuffs on Tawny.

"Nah, this is at least two hundred dollars," the first officer said.

"That ain't mine!" Tawny shouted. Her bandana and a couple of her braids had come off.

"And I guess this American Express card is yours, huh," he pulled the card closer, "Mrs. Huffmeister?" he sarcastically replied. "Yep, you look like your last name is Huffmeister. Who'd you steal this credit card from?"

"That ain't mine either. I been set up. It's a conspiracy. Entrapment. You just doing this 'cause I'm black!" she shouted as Officer Raybo dragged her to the patrol car.

"So are you coming down to file charges?" the other officer asked David.

"You'd better believe I am," David said. He turned to Rachel.

"Go on. I'll stay here with D.J. until you get back," Rachel said.

David kissed her on the cheek. "Thank you, Sis. I owe you big time."

"You don't owe me anything. Just make sure they lock her up. If for no other reason than to get her some help."

David's smile faded and Rachel could see that underneath the anger, he still genuinely cared for Tawny.

"You did what you had to do," she tried to reassure him.

"I did. I did." He took off toward his car, still muttering, "I did," like he was trying to convince himself.

chapter 38

The sounds of "Joy to the World" filled the small meeting room at Zion Hill Missionary Baptist Church. Although it was unusually warm for December—74 degrees—there was still a festive atmosphere in the room.

The girls had spent the past hour hanging Christmas decorations, moving furniture, and setting up the food for the Good Girlz Christmas party, scheduled to get under way in less than ten minutes.

Rachel stood outside the doorway watching Angel, Camille, Alexis, and Jasmine as they joked around. She tried to compose herself before she walked in. This was their day; their families would be there, so she had to put on a good front and set all of her own problems aside.

"It's so nice to see my girls working together," she said as she entered the room. She looked at her watch. "You've been here, what, a whole hour and nobody's started arguing. I must be in the Twilight Zone."

She took pride in how well the girls were getting along. It was very different from the way they had bickered when they first started with the group.

"Oh, Miss Rachel's got jokes," Jasmine said, cutting her eyes.

Rachel playfully pinched Jasmine's cheek. "You know I am so proud of you girls." She looked around the room. "And you all have done such a wonderful job decorating this room."

"Yeah, we wanted the party to be really nice," Alexis said as she hung another string of garland across the window. Besides the seven-foot tree and the garlands across all the windows, there was a diverse array of angels and other ornaments positioned all over the room. Ribbons added the final touch to the podium in front.

"I love Christmastime," Rachel said. "When I was growing up my mom used to go crazy at Christmas. She would buy us so much stuff and my daddy would always fuss, but he never made her take any of the stuff back."

"I wish I could've met your mother," Angel said as she sat down to massage her feet. "She seemed like she was really nice."

"She was. I just didn't appreciate her until she was gone."

"How did your mom die?" Camille asked.

Rachel's eyes misted up. "She had a heart attack when I was

nineteen. I always wonder—if my brothers and I hadn't made her life so hard, would her heart have given out? It was like the stress of dealing with our problems made her heart weak." She gazed out the window as the room grew silent. She wished her mother was here to give her advice on how to handle this situation with Lester.

She caught herself and snapped out of her daze. "Look at me. This is not a sad occasion. Today is a good day. This is a celebration of how far we've come. Your families are coming and we are here to celebrate the progress you've made."

"I hate to interrupt this tender moment here." Everyone turned toward Lester, who had just walked in the room. "But I wanted to see if you guys were ready."

Rachel forced a smile. The girls were all staring at her so she had to remain upbeat, not letting on that anything was wrong. "We're fine."

Lester looked a little surprised that she was even speaking to him, but Rachel hoped he could read the expression behind her eyes, the one that told him she still wanted to wring his neck.

"Wow, you all have done a good job," Lester said, looking around the room and trying to get Rachel's gaze off of him.

"Thank you," Alexis responded.

"And we're ready just in time, because here comes your mother and sister, Angel," Rachel said.

Rachel didn't know how she made it through the party because her heart was still in so much pain. But she managed to put up a good front and everything went off without a hitch.

Afterward, Rachel said good-bye to everyone's families. She was grateful that she was taking the girls to a hotel for a slumber party—one room for herself and one for the girls. She'd dropped Nia and Jordan off at her dad's and was looking forward to some alone time to think and get her head together. After all, she did have a divorce to plan.

Lester stood off to the side like a pitiful puppy dog as they packed up their things to head to the hotel. She refused to even look at him as she made her way out of the room.

An hour later, Rachel was snuggled up under the comforter at the Hilton, eating Häagen-Dazs ice cream and flipping through the channels. She had gotten the girls settled in and planned to spend the rest of the night wallowing in self-pity. She stopped channel surfing when she saw the movie *War of the Roses* on HBO. "Just what I need," she mumbled as she popped a spoonful of ice cream in her mouth.

Rachel rolled her eyes when she heard a knock on the door. *Why did I think I'd actually get some peace and quiet?* She'd ordered the girls pizza and drinks and thought that would keep them occupied.

She set her ice cream on the nightstand and threw back the covers. "What do you all want?" she moaned as she swung the door open. "I thought you—"

"I want you," Lester replied, a desperate look in his eyes.

"Why are you here?" she demanded.

"I'm here to save my marriage."

"Whatever, Lester. You should've thought about that before you went off and had an affair."

"What can I do to make this right?"

A curious couple walked by, obviously trying to figure out the drama. Rachel huffed and motioned for Lester to come inside. No use having *all* her business in the street.

"Turn back the hands of time and don't cheat on me." She sat down on the king-size bed and flipped off the TV.

"If I could, I would."

"Lester, why are you here?" she repeated.

"I told you, to save my marriage."

She sighed. "It can't be saved. It's over."

"I don't believe that." He sat down on the edge of the bed.

"I do." Rachel stared him straight in the eyes. "I want a divorce."

Lester hesitated, obviously not expecting her to say that. "You can't mean that."

"Yes, I can, and I do. I don't trust you and if I can't trust you, you can't trust me." She folded her arms across her chest and glared at her husband.

"What does that mean?"

"It means what it means."

"Have you been with someone else?" he asked, his voice cracking.

"You lost the right to ask me that question when you had sex with another woman."

Lester looked like he wanted to cry as he massaged his temple.

"It doesn't feel good, does it, Lester?" She stood up and towered over him. "It doesn't feel good to even think the person you swore to love until death did you part is giving her body to someone else. Letting another man touch her, love her." She was taunting him now, but she didn't care. "Does it bother you to picture her moaning with pleasure? Does it feel like someone is tearing your heart out?"

Lester sat up, his eyes watering. "Was it Bobby?"

She replied, a smug look on her face. "Don't worry about who it was." Rachel didn't know why she was doing this. She had never planned to make him think she had been with someone else, but since he went there, why not? She wanted him to know her pain. "Maybe it was Bobby," she said. "Maybe it was somebody new."

Lester suddenly jumped up and grabbed her by the arms. "Stop it! Stop trying to hurt me," he said as he shook her.

Rachel gritted her teeth as she glared at her husband. "Like you hurt me?" she told him through clenched teeth. "Get your hands off of me before I scream at the top of my lungs and have your cheating ass thrown in jail."

Lester realized how tightly he was clutching Rachel and let her go. "I'm sorry." He stared at her, his eyes welling with tears. "I'm sorry for everything." He headed to the door, then stopped and turned back toward her. "I messed up, Rachel. I did. But I'm not going to lose my family. I *can't* lose my family. You can try to pay me back all you want, but I'll still never give up on you. I moved back home tonight. I'll sleep in the guest room, but I'm not letting you go without a fight."

He walked out of the room and Rachel felt her stomach

sink, the smugness disappearing from her face. Why wasn't revenge—or even just talk of revenge—giving her the vindicated feeling she needed? How was she going to deal with him being back in the house? Why wouldn't he just give up and leave her alone? She didn't even attempt to figure out those questions as she climbed back into bed and tried to let sleep help ease some of her pain.

chapter 39

Simon was smiling ear to ear. Rachel wanted to believe it was because they were all there—with the exception of David, who was at home with D.J.—celebrating Simon's birthday at Johnny Carrino's Italian restaurant. But somehow, she couldn't help but feel the woman sitting across from him, shooting him googly eyes, was the real reason he was smiling.

"Mrs. Brenda, we're so happy you could join us," Jonathan said.

"There's no place else I'd rather be," she replied, not taking her eyes off Simon. She finally turned to Jonathan, "than here helping Sim . . . I mean, Pastor Jackson celebrate his sixty-fifth birthday."

"Mrs. Brenda, why don't you just go ahead and call my dad

Simon? By now, we all know you're more than just any old member to him," Rachel remarked sarcastically.

Everyone glared at Rachel. Even Jordan and Nia, sensing the tension, stopped playing and stared also. Rachel had been in a foul mood for the last two days. Lester had indeed moved back home and although he tried his best to stay out of her way, just having him in the same house put her in a horrible mood.

"Now, Rachel," Simon began, "I've had just about enough—"

Brenda held up a hand and cut him off. "No, Simon. I can handle this." She leaned into the table. "Rachel, you know I have nothing but respect for you—as first lady of my church and as the daughter of the man I love."

Both Rachel's and Jonathan's eyes grew wide as Brenda continued. "But let me be clear, in order for me to continue to give respect, I must get respect." Her tone got gentler as she placed her hand on top of Rachel's. "Now, I understand how hard this may be for you, but Loretta died, Simon didn't. And no one can ever take her place. I wouldn't even try, couldn't if I wanted to." She looked at Simon. "But his heart is big enough that he found a little room in it for me. I just ask that you let him have that. Let *us* have that."

Rachel felt her eyes pooling. She had to admit she admired Brenda's spunk. And there was no denying how happy her father seemed lately. Suddenly she felt like crap.

Jonathan spoke up. "Mrs. Brenda, I don't think my sister means to give you a hard time. It's just—it's a little harder for her than the rest of us, to accept my father loving anyone other than my mother."

Brenda replied, "That's understandable. That's why I've been patient. Why I'll continue to be patient."

Rachel looked back and forth between her father and Brenda. "I'm sorry. It's not just you, Mrs. Brenda. I . . . I have a lot on my mind."

Brenda nodded understandingly as Simon squeezed Rachel's arm. "No need for apologies, baby girl." He sipped the last of his coffee. "This has been a wonderful birthday celebration, but you know I'm an old man, and it's getting late."

Jonathan signed the receipt, leaving the waitress a hefty tip before they headed out to the parking lot.

Outside, Brenda released Simon's hand and turned to Rachel. "Are we okay?"

Rachel smiled and nodded. She knew she was acting like a child and it was time to let that go. "We're okay."

They hugged each other.

"And whatever it is that has your heart so heavy, know that you're in my prayers," Brenda said.

"That's what I like to see, one big happy . . ." Simon's words trailed off as he watched the black car slow down in front of them. Rachel, Jonathan, and Brenda turned and watched the car as well. The passenger window eased down and it didn't quite register what was happening until a black barrel came out the window and the sounds of gunfire pierced the air.

Jonathan grabbed Rachel and dove for the ground. Simon

did the same with Brenda as people scattered everywhere. The tires screeched as the car took off.

"Oh, my God!" Rachel screamed. "Jordan! Nia!" She scrambled to get up off the ground. "My babies." Rachel looked around frantically. She saw Jordan crouched down behind a car, his arms tightly around Nia. She raced toward them. "Oh, my God! Oh, my God!" She took both of them in her arms, crying uncontrollably.

Suddenly, Brenda screamed. "He's been hit! Help, somebody!"

"Do not move!" she told Jordan and Nia as she raced back over to Brenda, Simon, and Jonathan.

Chaos reigned as people started piling out of the restaurant.

"Who was hit?" Rachel looked down at Jonathan, who was staring at her father in a daze. "Oh, no!" Rachel dropped to the ground next to her father. "Daddy!"

Brenda held his head. "Simon, please, wake up. Hang on. Help is on the way."

Rachel saw blood forming underneath her father and she almost passed out. "No, no, no."

Although it couldn't have been more than five minutes, it seemed like forever before the paramedics arrived.

"What happened?" a police officer asked as the paramedics went to work on her father.

"My father . . ." Jonathan said, shaking his head. "Somebody tried to kill us . . . my father . . . he was hit."

The officer pulled out a pad and started writing.

"Is he going to make it?" Brenda sobbed.

Suddenly, Simon's eyes opened. He grimaced in pain. "Wh . . . what happened?"

"Shhhh, don't try to talk," Brenda said.

"Did s . . . somebody shoot me?" Simon struggled to ask.

"Sir, I need you to save your energy," a paramedic said as they eased him on the stretcher. "Luckily, the bullet just barely grazed your shoulder. You cut your head pretty bad when you hit the ground."

Rachel looked at the paramedics in disbelief. "So he's going to be all right?"

The paramedic examined Simon's head. "Yeah, this cut is pretty bad, but nothing a few stitches won't heal. It's a miracle that bullet whizzed right by his shoulder. Because two inches over and . . ."

Simon shook his head. "It wouldn't have been pretty." He tried to sit up but the pain quickly caused him to fall back against the stretcher. "But that wasn't no miracle. That was the armor of God watching out for me." He forced himself to smile at Brenda.

"Amen," she replied.

The paramedics wheeled Simon to the ambulance. "We're taking him to Sugar Land Methodist. One of you can ride with him."

Rachel and Brenda both stepped up at the same time. Brenda looked at Rachel with a plea in her eyes. Rachel sighed, stepped back, and said, "We'll see you at the hospital."

Brenda hugged her before jumping into the ambulance with Simon.

chapter 40

David walked back and forth in the living room, shaking his head. "A drive-by shooting? In Sugar Land?"

"Like nice areas don't have drive-bys," Rachel sarcastically replied. "People just aren't safe anywhere. This just doesn't make sense."

They were in Simon's living room, going over the shooting for the hundredth time. Simon only had to spend one night in the hospital. He'd been released this morning and was now resting upstairs. Brenda hadn't left his side since the shooting.

"You think Tawny would do something like this, or have one of her friends do it?" Rachel asked. She'd been playing out all the possible scenarios.

David shook his head. "Naw, she's still in jail. Besides, she doesn't have the money or the power to pull off something like this from behind bars."

"Well, I want to know if this was random, or do we have to walk around in fear," Rachel said.

"So what are the police saying?" David asked.

"They aren't any help," Rachel replied. She leaned forward in her seat and rubbed her tired eyes.

"It had to be random," Jonathan said, snapping out of his deep thought. "Unless . . ."

"Unless what?" Rachel asked.

Jonathan got up and walked over to the fireplace. He had debated saying anything but it was the only reasonable explanation he could think of. "Unless the bullet was meant for me."

"You?" Rachel asked. "Why would someone try to shoot you?"

"This whole custody suit. It's gotten pretty ugly," he said sadly.

"So? You think Angela would stoop to murder? I mean, I know she's changed, but come on," Rachel scoffed.

"Maybe not Angela," Jonathan replied. "But her cousin Buster has been in and out of jail and I know he can't stand me. A drive-by wouldn't be beneath him."

Rachel jumped up and raced over to the telephone.

"What are you doing?"

"I'm calling the cops." She started punching in the numbers.

Jonathan rushed to the phone and quickly pushed the button to terminate the call. "And tell them what, exactly?"

"That your ex-wife is trying to off you."

"You don't have any proof of that."

"Well, are we supposed to just let her get away with this?" Rachel almost stamped her foot, she was so frustrated.

Jonathan sighed. "I could be way off base."

David scratched his head. "Rachel, what about you, you piss anybody off lately?"

She flashed him an incredulous look. "Me? Please. I have a lot of people who don't like me, but nobody who would try to kill me."

"You know what, this is just our imagination working over-time," Jonathan finally said. "Nobody tried to kill us. We were just in the wrong place at the wrong time. We just need to be thankful that no one was seriously hurt."

Rachel looked at her brother skeptically. "You can try to convince yourself of that all you want, but I'm not buying it," she said. "And if Angela or her people tried to kill you, I want them thrown in jail."

"I second that," David said.

Jonathan stared at his siblings, regretting he'd said anything. Somehow he just knew that things were about to get really ugly.

chapter 41

"Rachel, I'm going to ask you one more time not to do this." Lester stood in the doorway of his home, trying to stop his wife from leaving.

"And I'm going to ask you one more time to move out of my way," she replied, her tone hostile. She was still mad that he was here. She'd tried unsuccessfully to get him to leave, but he refused to go until they had tried every possible thing to work out their problems.

"Don't we have enough issues of our own? Why are you getting all up in your brother's business?"

She tossed her hair back out of her face. She was not going to let him get her worked up. She'd already consulted a divorce attorney and planned to file the paperwork tomorrow to start the process of removing him from her life. "First of all, when Angela's people took a shot at my brother, they also took a shot at me and my children." The police hadn't confirmed anything but ever since Jonathan raised the possibility, Rachel had been more and more certain that Angela was behind the shooting.

"Why don't you let the police handle it?"

"Trust me, I've already been to the cops. Now, please move out of my way."

"Can we please talk about our problems?" Lester begged.

"As far as I'm concerned, we don't have a problem. Not anymore."

"So, you're still on this divorce thing?" Lester softly said.

"I never got off it."

"We haven't had a chance to talk about this."

"There's nothing to talk about. Just because you forced your way back into our home doesn't mean everything is fine. Besides, in case you haven't noticed, I've been kind of busy trying to make sure the person who shot at my family is punished."

"I'm not undermining the seriousness of that, but even the police said they don't think the gunman was aiming for you all."

"That was before they knew about the threats Angela's relatives made to my brother." She pushed him aside. "Move, Lester. The detectives are supposed to be at her house in twenty minutes."

"Well, why are *you* going? Let them handle it. I just don't think you need to be caught up in any of this."

Rachel spun on Lester. "What part of 'I don't care what you

think' do you not get?" She glared at him like she wanted to say more, but then decided against it and stomped out the door.

Fifteen minutes later, Rachel was sitting in her car in front of Angela's house. The detectives hadn't yet arrived. She'd specifically been told to stay away. Yeah, right. She wouldn't rest until someone paid for trying to kill her family.

Rachel scrunched up her nose when she noticed Angela and her mother standing in the front yard pointing at her. They finally walked over to her car.

"May I help you?" Angela asked.

Rachel knew she probably should just drive away but her blood was starting to boil. She stepped out of the car.

"I just wanted to be here when they come to arrest you," she said.

Angela looked at her mother, then back at Rachel. "Arrest me? For what?"

"Attempted murder. Accessory to attempted murder. One of them. We know it was you—or one of your hood rat relatives—who opened fire on me and my kids, my daddy, and Jon last week." Rachel crossed her arms and tried to study Angela's reaction.

"What in Christ's name are you talking about?" Mrs. Brooks asked.

"Attempted murder?" Angela asked. "Someone tried to kill you all?"

"Don't act all innocent," Rachel said.

"Rachel, seriously, I have no idea what you're talking about," Angela said.

Rachel threw her a "whatever" look.

"Is Jonathan still alive?" Mrs. Brooks asked.

"Of course he is," Rachel replied. "He wasn't even hit."

"Well, that proves we didn't do it," Mrs. Brooks said snidely. "Because if it had been us, we wouldn't have missed."

"Mother!" Angela snapped.

Mrs. Brooks rolled her eyes. "I'm not going to pretend I'm concerned about somebody trying to kill Jonathan Jackson. Shoot, I just wish I had the courage to do it myself."

It was Angela's turn to roll her eyes. "Mother, please go in the house."

Before Mrs. Brooks could respond, a black Oldsmobile pulled up. Two men in navy suits stepped out. Rachel recognized the driver as the detective she had filed the report with.

"Mrs. Adams, what are you doing here?" he said.

"Harassing us," Mrs. Brooks replied. "Can't you arrest her?"

"Your daughter is the one who needs to be arrested," Rachel snapped.

The second officer stepped up. Everyone immediately got quiet. "Ladies," he said, turning to Angela and her mother, "why don't you two come inside with me and Detective Reid and answer a couple of questions. We'll be out of your hair in no time."

"Mrs. Adams, go home," Detective Reid admonished. "We'll let you know if anything develops."

They all started walking toward Angela's house. She stopped and turned back to Rachel. "Is . . . is Simon okay?"

Rachel glared at Angela. Those definitely weren't the eyes of a killer. "Yeah, he's going to be fine."

"That's good," she softly replied, before saying, "I didn't try and kill Jonathan, or anyone else for that matter."

Rachel was surprised, but all of a sudden, she believed her. But if Angela wasn't behind the drive-by shooting, then who was?

chapter 42

Angela knew she shouldn't be doing this, but no matter what some judge said, she would never feel comfortable with her son around Jonathan.

After that mess with the police showing up at her house last week, she probably should've stayed as far away as possible from Zion Hill and the Jackson clan. But she couldn't help herself; this was her child, for Christ's sake.

Last night was Chase's first overnight visit, and she'd been a nervous wreck all night. She knew they'd be here at church this morning, so she had to come see how Chase was doing.

Angela shifted in the pew, then pushed her sunglasses up on her nose before pulling her big floppy hat down to hide her face. The sight of Jonathan laughing and smiling as he introduced Chase to everyone at church made her sick to her stomach. Maybe she should've just taken her son and run. But what kind of life would that have been for Chase?

"Excuse me. Is someone sitting there?"

Angela looked up at the elderly woman trying to take the seat next to her. The robust woman looked like she wanted Angela to move down and let her sit on the end. But Angela wasn't moving. She needed to be on the end so she could keep a close eye on Jonathan and her child. She wasn't trying to be rude, but she was on a mission.

"You gon' move down or you want me to step my arthritic legs over you?" the woman said.

Angela didn't respond, but did move her legs to the side to let the woman pass.

Fifteen minutes later when Rachel asked visitors to stand and be greeted, the elderly woman stood up. Angela knew she was supposed to greet the woman, but she wasn't in church for that. She folded her arms and looked away.

"I guess you just ain't gon' say nothing to me, huh?" the old lady asked. "If this is how black folks act in Houston, I know I need to go back to Sweet Poke. Can't even speak to nobody in the Lord's house."

"Mama Tee, what are you doing here?" A short, plus-size woman with wild, reddish mini dreadlocks stopped at the end of their aisle, reached over Angela, and hugged the old woman.

"Hey, Shereen, baby," the woman said. "I'm just here with

Nikki, you know she goes here now. We're in town visiting my brother, and you know I had to come to church."

"That's right. Rae did say you'd be here this weekend. I'll have to call her."

Angela wondered if they were going to hold a whole conversation over her.

"Who's this?" Shereen motioned to Angela.

"Somebody that needs Jesus," Mama Tee loudly responded. "She ain't with me."

"Oh." Shereen flashed a smile. Angela looked away. She was glad when they said their good-byes and Shereen returned to her seat.

By the time they got to the sermon, Angela was just ready for service to be over. She wanted the whole day to be over so she could get her child back.

Mama Tee leaned in to Angela. "Let it go, chile," she whispered.

"Excuse me?"

"Let whatever is eating you go. You letting the devil fill your heart. Let go and let God." She gently patted Angela's leg and turned her attention back to Lester, who was preaching about, of all things, forgiveness.

Angela felt tears forming as she actually began to focus on Lester's message. Would she ever be able to forgive Jonathan? Shoot, could she even forgive God, for that matter? Angela could count on one hand the number of times she'd been to church over the last seven years. She was angry with God and just hadn't been able to get over it.

"I'm gon' pray for you," Mama Tee whispered as Lester wrapped up his sermon. " 'Cause I got a feeling you can't pray for yourself right about now."

Angela nodded, suddenly regretting that she'd been so mean to the woman. She managed to concentrate on the rest of the service, although she continued to steal glances at Jonathan and Chase. The little boy seemed to be adapting well. Too well, in fact.

Most of the congregation had left when Jonathan and Chase finally emerged. Jonathan was talking and laughing with some man as they walked out of the church. Angela straightened up against her car and narrowed her eyes at the sight of Jonathan and the man. Chase was right behind them. She felt her fury building as she watched Jonathan and the man together. The way they were being so attentive, the way they were looking at each other. And with her son standing right there!

Angela could no longer contain her anger. She raced across the parking lot and didn't stop until she was hitting Jonathan in the chest.

"I can't believe you have my child out here witnessing this nasty behavior!" She didn't know what had come over her, but she just kept swinging. "I knew this would happen. You're going to scar my son for life!"

By this time, Chase was crying and screaming, Jonathan was trying to shield himself from her blows, and the man he was with was trying to grab her. Several other people had gathered outside as well. No one could seem to get through to

Angela. She was screaming as tears ran down her cheeks, "I hate you! I hate you!"

"Angela! What are you doing?" Her cousin, Melanie, was in front of her now.

"He . . . Jonathan . . . I knew he was going to do this," Angela sobbed as she fell in her cousin's arms. "He's out here parading his lover in front of my child! He's going to make my child like him."

Angela ignored the crowd gathered around her. She only focused on Chase, who was clutching Jonathan's leg, fear all over his face.

"Come here, baby. Get away from him," Angela said.

"Angela, what is wrong with you?" Jonathan demanded.

"Angela. Why don't we go inside."

Angela looked over to find Rachel by her side. She was surprised by the sincere look on Rachel's face. But she wasn't fooled. They were all in this together, the whole Jackson clan.

"Get away from me. I can't stand any of you," Angela cried. "Chase, come on."

Jonathan stepped in front of Chase to stop him from leaving.

Angela glared at Jonathan. "Let my child go."

"Angela, please calm down."

"Don't you dare talk to me. I will not have my child witnessing you and your lovers!" She motioned dramatically toward the man Jonathan had been talking to.

Jonathan shook his head, motioning for the man to come over. "Angela, I want you to meet—"

"I don't want to meet him!"

Jonathan took a deep breath. "Angela, this is my cousin, Jeffrey. He's just visiting for the weekend."

Angela stared in disbelief. "Your cousin?"

Rachel stepped up closer to her. "*Our* cousin. My dad's brother's son. Ask Melanie." Rachel's voice was surprisingly gentle.

Angela looked at Melanie, who still had a look of horror on her face. She slowly nodded.

Angela buried her face in her hands. "Oh, my God. I am so sorry."

Rachel put her arm around Angela. "Come on inside for a minute," she whispered.

"I'll take her home," Melanie snapped.

Rachel looked at her. "Please, Melanie. Let's just get her inside for a minute."

Melanie glanced around at the crowd and must've decided that wasn't such a bad idea. She followed them in.

chapter 43

Jonathan inhaled deeply and knocked on the door to Rachel's office. Jeffrey had taken Chase for ice cream so Jonathan could make sure Angela was all right.

The whole scenario had caught him totally off guard. Angela was like a crazy woman. It made him realize the depth of her pain.

"Hey, Rach. It's me, Jonathan."

"Hold on," Rachel called out. He heard some mumbling, then Rachel opened the door.

"Is she okay?" Jonathan whispered.

Rachel's eyes were red as if she'd been crying as well. "She's okay."

"Can I talk to her?"

"Maybe now's not a good time," Rachel said. That surprised Jonathan; normally she wouldn't have been so sympathetic to Angela.

"No, it's all right. Let him in," Angela said from behind the door.

Rachel eased the door open. Angela was sitting on the sofa, a box of Kleenex in her lap.

"Melanie, how about we give them a moment," Rachel said.

Melanie flashed a skeptical look at Rachel. "You sure about this?" she asked Angela.

Angela nodded and Melanie got up and walked outside.

Jonathan waited until they closed the door. "Angela . . ."

"This is so embarrassing. I'm sorry," she said, not looking up at him.

Jonathan sat down next to her. "Don't be."

"Where's Chase?"

"My cousin took him for ice cream."

"Is he okay?"

"Yeah. Worried about you, that's all."

"I can't believe I freaked like that," she said, finally looking up.

"Angela, don't worry about it. I . . . I know you've been through a lot and you probably just . . . just let your imagination run rampant."

She nodded as tears started running down her cheeks again.

"Angela, I know I had some issues with myself and I hurt you in the process of working those out. And I'm going to be honest, I think as long as I have a happy, stable home, Chase will be fine."

She opened her mouth like she was about to protest. Jonathan held up his finger and cut her off. "But, I told you, out of respect for you, I will not bring anyone . . . any man I'm involved with around our son. Honestly, that's not my focus right now anyway. The only thing I want is to build a relationship with Chase."

"I don't want my son to be gay."

Jonathan exhaled. "Angela, it's not contagious. I just want to be a father to my child. I promise I won't play with dolls or play hopscotch with him. We'll do manly stuff like football, fighting, and fishing. How's that?" he said, trying to lighten the mood.

A small smile crossed her face. "Did that sound as stupid to you as it did to me?"

"Yeah, it did." Jonathan nodded.

Angela got up and started pacing back and forth. "Jonathan, you will have to bear with me. This isn't easy. You hurt me so bad that I just shut down. I never dealt with your betrayal. I shut out my family. I shut out God. I didn't know how to deal with the pain. The only person I allowed into my heart was Chase."

"I know. And I never want to take that from you. I couldn't even if I tried. But please, just let me have a little bit of his heart. I promise you, I'll guard it with my life."

Angela nodded. "I'm tired of running, tired of fighting, tired of hurting. I just want life to return to normal—whatever that is. So I'll try, Jonathan. That's all I can promise you."

He stood up. "Can you promise me another thing?"

She looked at him with raised eyebrows.

"Don't turn away from God. Don't let me turn you away from God."

She smiled gently. "I know I need to rebuild my relationship with God." She turned to stare out the window at the large cross that towered at the front of the church. "So I guess I can promise that, too."

"That's all I can ask." Jonathan wanted desperately to take her into his arms and hug her. He stared at her back before slowly walking up to her and putting his arms around her waist. Her shoulders sank as she inhaled deeply.

"I will always love you, Angela," Jonathan whispered.

"But not like I need to be loved," she whispered back. She took another deep breath, then turned to face him. Her eyes were filled with tears. "Never like I need to be loved."

Jonathan was just about to respond when the office door swung open.

"Get your grimy paws off her, you sick pervert!"

Angela immediately backed up. "Mother!"

Mrs. Brooks stormed over and stood in front of her daughter. "You disgusting bastard! You're trying to lure her back to you just so you can break her heart all over again!"

Mrs. Brooks swung her purse and hit Jonathan upside his head.

"Mother!" Angela screamed again as she grabbed Mrs. Brooks's arm.

"Don't 'Mother' me!" She spun on Angela. "Why would you let him touch you? After everything he's done."

Before anyone could say anything else, Rachel came running into the office, out of breath, Melanie close behind her. "Jonathan, I'm sorry," Rachel said. "She came barreling into the church and got back here before I could stop her."

"And thank God I did! He was about to seduce my daughter once again." Mrs. Brooks pushed Angela back. "You are a disgrace before God," she growled to Jonathan.

Angela moved around in front of her mother. "Mother, what are you doing here?"

"Sister Hicks called me and told me Jonathan was at church with his lover and you saw it and went ballistic. I raced right over here." She turned back to Jonathan. "And not a moment too soon."

"Mrs. Brooks, please calm down," Rachel said.

"And you." She wagged her purse at Rachel. "Don't you dare preach to me. Just a family full of deviants!"

"Enough, Mother!" Angela snapped. "This is ridiculous. Yes, I tripped out. But it was uncalled for. Just like this drama you're causing now."

Mrs. Brooks put her hand to her chest in shock. "What has he done to you?"

Watching her mother standing there, acting like a plumb idiot fool, confirmed for Angela that it was time to let the past go. "Mother, like it or not, Jonathan is Chase's father. We have to find a way to all get along."

"So now you're okay with him being a booty bumper?" Mrs. Brooks said, her voice laced with disbelief.

Jonathan had had enough. "Mrs. Brooks, I understand your anger because I know I hurt Angela. But this is between me and her. My sexuality is none of your business and I would appreciate it if you stopped with these derogatory remarks. I'm going to see my son. I'm going to build a relationship with my son. And there's not a thing you can do about it."

"He's right, Mother," Angela added.

Mrs. Brooks's eyes began to water. "I don't believe this." She glared at Angela. "When he brings his deviant behavior around Chase, don't say I didn't warn you." With that, she spun around and stomped out of the room.

As she left, Jonathan noticed Sister Hicks and Birdie Mae Canton peeking into the office. "Ooo-weeee. This is better than my soaps," Birdie Mae said.

Jonathan shook his head in disgust and slammed the door.

chapter 44

Rachel was hoping for an uneventful evening. It had been three days since that madness at church with Angela and her mother. But one good thing had came out of it all: Angela and Jonathan had reached some type of understanding.

Rachel dropped her Bible on her desk as she flipped through her mail. There was a thank-you card from the Good Girlz for all she'd done. That reminded her, she needed to send Sister Morgan and the First Ladies Council a card because they had really helped her in her walk with God. She didn't think she'd ever be on their level, but they'd definitely helped her grow. And she definitely needed that strength now, because the rumor mills were running rampant.

Everybody had heard about her little fight with Mary

Richardson, although people still didn't know exactly what was behind the fight, nor did they remember Mary from the day she visited church. Rachel had heard everything from she caught the woman and Lester in his office having sex to the woman had slapped her as she walked down the hall.

She was just trying to deal with the rumors until she could work out the details of the divorce, start looking for a new church, and figure out what she was going to do about the Good Girlz.

The phone ringing interrupted her thoughts.

"Hello?"

"Sister Adams? It's Linda Morgan. I just called to check on you."

Rachel smiled. Linda always seemed to call right when she needed her most. Rachel hadn't shared the sordid details of Lester's infidelity with anyone but Twyla, but it was like Linda knew something was wrong. Maybe she'd heard the rumors, too.

"I'm fine, Sister Morgan. Just taking it one day at a time."

"Well, I don't want to get all in your business, but make sure you take it to God as well."

So she *had* heard something. Rachel wasn't in the mood to go into any details so she just said, "I hear you, Sister Morgan."

"Yeah, but do you hear God? I won't hold you, but just remember, there is a demon assigned to each of us. His sole purpose is to destroy that which brings us joy. Sometimes what we think is God talking to us is actually that demon. We have to pray and listen carefully to decipher God's voice," she said.

A look of confusion crossed Rachel's face. Where was that coming from? And just what was it supposed to mean? As far as she was concerned the only demon that had destroyed her marriage was Lester.

Rachel glanced over at the clock. Seven o'clock. "Sister Morgan, as always thanks for the encouraging words, but I need to get to a meeting."

"Okay. Just remember if you need me, I'm only a phone call away."

Rachel said her good-byes and hung up the phone. She wasn't in the mood to try and decipher what Linda was trying to tell her. Nor was she in the mood to go deal with Birdie Mae and the other women, but they had to meet after Bible study to plan the church's anniversary celebration. And since the youth were playing a big role in the celebration, Rachel wanted to make sure she was at the meeting, especially because it would probably be the last event she ever did with the church.

Rachel made her way into the sanctuary where she noticed several women in a circle at the pulpit. They were deep in prayer. Rachel couldn't make out who was in the circle, but she could tell Lester was in the center. She could hear Birdie Mae's scratchy voice.

" . . . And Lord, we know you are a faithful God. A forgiving God. Please cleanse this woman's soul and forgive her for her transgression."

Rachel wondered why Birdie Mae was praying and not Lester. Even still, she stopped and bowed her head as they finished the prayer.

"These and other blessings we ask in Your name. Amen," Birdie Mae said.

"Amen," Rachel mumbled as she made her way up to the front. She stopped in her tracks as the crowd began to disperse and she saw who was at the center of the prayer circle.

"What is she doing here?" Rachel said.

"Excuse me?" Birdie Mae said, turning to her.

"You talking about Mary here?" Sister Hicks said. "This is the lady that gave the testimony in church several weeks ago. She came again this evening seeking prayer. So we're praying for her."

Rachel just stood staring at Mary, who had a smirk on her face. Lester stood next to her, sweating bullets.

"I'm even thinking about joining. That is, if you all will have me," she said innocently.

"Of course we will," Sister Hicks said.

"Yeah, don't matter none to us that you white," Birdie Mae added. Several people cut their eyes at her. "What? She is white," Birdie Mae snapped.

"Yes, but the Lord is color-blind. We are all God's children," Sister Hicks said as she took Mary's hand. "And we sure would be honored to have you on our church roster. Ain't that right, Sister Adams?"

Rachel was still in the aisle, stunned at the audacity of this woman.

"Sister Adams, ain't that right?" Norma Jean Woodruff repeated.

Mary hooked her arm around Lester's. "After I heard Reverend Adams preach, I just knew this was the church home I'd been looking for."

"Amen. He is a marvelous preacher, ain't he?" Sister Hicks said.

"We just lucky to have him," Norma Jean echoed.

Rachel's chest started to heave. She turned and raced out of the sanctuary.

Inside her office, she paced back and forth, trying to keep her anger under control. "Do not act a fool. Do not act a fool," she muttered. Part of her wanted to drop to her knees and pray for the strength not to kill Mary and Lester. The other part wanted to go right into the sanctuary and kill both of them.

Lester eased her office door open. "Rachel?"

Rachel spun around. "Lester, if you know what's good for you, you will leave me alone."

Lester stepped into her office and closed the door behind him. "No."

"No?" These people wouldn't let her be sane. They would push and push and push until she snapped.

"Rachel, I had no idea she would be here."

"You know what? I'm so sick of that lame excuse. Nobody was forcing you to stand up in that circle praying with her."

"What would you suggest I do? Everyone put me on the spot. *She* put me on the spot. She asked me to stand there and pray for her. I was so in shock I couldn't even speak. That's why Birdie Mae was praying instead of me." Lester desperately wanted Rachel to believe him. "I mean, you can't blame them. None of them were there the day you and Mary got into it.

They don't know what happened between us. They think she's just some woman in need of prayer."

Rachel didn't care anymore. "You know what, Lester? I'm through. I can't do this." She couldn't help it. The tears started flowing. "I changed who I was for you, for these people around here. I'm sick of them and I'm sick of you."

"Rachel, what did you expect me to do?"

"I expected you to be faithful. To honor your commitment to me. That's what I expected! No, you might not have been able to control what happened tonight but you could have controlled being in this situation in the first place. If you had never brought her into our lives, we wouldn't have this problem. I wouldn't be hurting like I am now." She grabbed her purse.

"Where are you going?"

"Home. To pack. If you won't leave, I will. I can't do this." Rachel knew she couldn't wait for a divorce to go through now. She had to get out before she lost her mind.

Lester jumped in front of her. "Please let's work this out."

"I can't. Good-bye, Lester." Rachel stepped around him.

Lester followed her out, trying to talk to her. Rachel ignored him as she made her way to her car.

"I'm coming home, too. We need to talk about this."

"There is nothing for us to talk about. And don't bother coming home. Because I won't be there." Rachel got into her car and drove off.

chapter 45

Rachel stood outside of Bobby's house. She inhaled deeply, trying to shake off that voice that was telling her to turn around. She couldn't go to her father's because she was in no mood for a lecture. She didn't want to keep running hot and cold on Bobby, but right now, she just wanted familiar arms to comfort her.

Rachel ran her fingers through her hair, fluffing up the curls, then brushed down her prairie skirt and adjusted the turquoise belt that was wrapped snugly around her waist.

Bobby opened the door, a shocked look on his face. "Rachel, are you okay?" he said, wiping away a tear she didn't even realize was trickling down her cheek.

"I'm sorry to come here . . . I just needed to talk . . . to be around some . . ."

"Sshhhh," he said as he pulled her inside. He eased her down on the sofa. "Tell me what's wrong."

Rachel couldn't hold it in. She laid her head on his shoulder and began sobbing. "My marriage is over," she whimpered.

Bobby held her, stroking her hair for several minutes. "Everything will be okay," he whispered. He gently lifted her chin. "You'll get through this," he said, gazing into her eyes.

Rachel was about to respond when Bobby slowly leaned into her. She felt herself sinking as his lips met hers. Just as his tongue tried to find its way inside her mouth, she pulled away. "Bobby, I . . . I didn't come here to lead you on." Rachel couldn't deny the attraction she felt, but she knew anything she did right now would be out of pure revenge. Revenge and lust.

"I'm sorry, Rachel. I guess I just got caught up." He stood, trying to compose himself. "Can I get you something to drink?"

"Some chardonnay would be good."

Bobby nodded as he walked into the kitchen. Rachel closed her eyes, trying to get her thoughts together. Why had she come here again?

"Man, you've come a long way from your Boones Farm days." Bobby laughed, as he returned with two glasses. Rachel could tell he was trying to lighten the mood as he handed her a glass and sat down. "So do you want to tell me what happened?"

Rachel fingered her glass. "Not really."

Thankfully, he didn't push her.

"Why don't you tell me what happened to you and Shante?" Maybe if she could get her mind off her own problems, she'd feel better.

Bobby leaned back and sipped his wine. "You know I was never over you. You knew it when you showed up at my wedding and kissed me. I know you could feel I wasn't over you in that kiss."

Rachel remembered that kiss well. He had definitely kissed her back. But when he'd gone ahead and married Shante, she figured she'd imagined the whole thing.

"As precious as Nia is, you hurt me so bad with Tony—I thought the only way I could heal from that was to move on. But I never could. I never could get you out of my system. Shante knew that. It's why she left."

Rachel was speechless. She'd never known Bobby still loved her like that. "So, have you filed for divorce?" she finally asked.

"Yeah, we've begun the process."

Rachel weighed his words. What did that mean for her? Especially now that she was divorcing Lester, too? "Bobby, why are you doing this, telling me that you love me?"

"Because I do. I should have told you a long time ago." He scooted closer to her. He leaned in and began kissing her again, and this time she didn't stop him as he rubbed his hand up her back under her shirt.

All kinds of emotions were running through her. The battle between good and evil resumed in her head. *What are you doing? What's good for the goose is good for the gander. Don't let Lester's infidelities steal your commitment to God. Girl, get your groove on!* Rachel felt like her head was about to explode. She tried to pull back. Bobby started kissing her neck.

"Rachel, I have dreamed about this day, holding you in my arms. I just want to be with you. I have never stopped loving you," he moaned.

Rachel felt her resolve weaken and the good voice dancing in her head started to fade.

Bobby had just unfastened her bra when they heard a loud crash. Both of them jumped off the sofa: a flowerpot had crashed through the window. "I see you in there, you no-good dog!"

Bobby jumped up and raced over to his window. "Shante?" he said.

"Open the door!" she screamed.

Bobby stood stunned for a minute.

"Open the door or I will start screaming so all the neighbors will know you're in there with your whore!"

Bobby sighed, then went to open the door. Rachel stood back in horror, not believing she was in this situation.

"What are you doing here?" Bobby snarled. "You gave me your key back and said we were through."

"You are still my husband. Until the paperwork is signed, you are still my husband. The question is why the hell is she here?"

Rachel discreetly tried to fasten her bra. She hated to admit it, but Shante actually looked ten times better than she used to. She'd lost about forty pounds and wore a tight jogging suit. Her weave was loosely curled and hanging down her back. Her makeup was flawless. She definitely had dressed up to come over here.

"I better get going," Rachel said.

"Yeah, tramp, you better get going." Shante stepped into the room and stopped just inches from Rachel's face.

Rachel took a deep breath. "Shante, get out of my face."

"Or what? You gon' key my car, cut my utilities off, jump me, or better yet, try to kill me with a butcher knife?" She spun on Bobby. "I can't believe you. We are still married, you know."

"Shante, you're the one who made it clear we were over." Bobby sighed.

"And this is the reason why," she said, dramatically flinging her arm toward Rachel. "You just couldn't wait to go running back to her, could you?" She turned back to Rachel. "Where's your husband, the good reverend? Does he know you're over here committing adultery with your baby's daddy?"

"Shante, you need to leave," Bobby warned.

"Bobby, *I'm* going to leave. I'll talk to you later." Rachel grabbed her purse and headed toward the door.

"Oh, since you all saved and sanctified now, you wanna go run and hide. You ain't fooling nobody. You still the same worthless piece of trash you were seven years ago. That's why don't nobody at your own church like you. That's why your husband was cheating on you!" Shante spat.

Bobby looked stunned. Rachel spun around, her eyes shooting fire. "So I guess your bigmouthed sister told you that?"

Shante laughed. "Nope, Layla didn't have to tell me anything. You wanna know how I know about Mary?" She sneered.

It was Rachel's turn to look surprised. *How did Shante know her name?*

Shante folded her arms and smiled. "Mary is a friend of a friend who will do anything for a couple of dollars—including screwing the most faithful preacher in town."

"What?"

"You're not the only one who can play dirty. Do you think I didn't know about all the evil, underhanded stuff you did trying to get Bobby not to marry me? Do you think I was going to let you wreck my marriage and get away with it?"

"Are you kidding me? That was seven years ago!" Rachel couldn't believe her ears. Lester had been set up?

"I don't care if it was seventeen years ago. I told you you would get yours," Shante told her.

"Are you saying you hired someone to seduce her husband?" Bobby asked, his voice laced with disbelief.

"That's exactly what I'm saying. It didn't take much because poor little Lester was so unfulfilled at home. All Mary had to do was show him a little attention and he was all hers. Hell, she even stopped charging me because she was digging him herself." Shante stood with a proud look on her face.

Bobby shook his head. "I don't believe you, Shante!"

"You don't believe *me*? After all this heifer did? She's lucky that's all I did."

"That was years ago, Shante," Bobby protested.

"Oh, she might not have directly done anything to me in the last seven years. But she's the reason my marriage failed. She's haunted us from the day we met. Do you think I'm stupid? You've compared me and everything about me to her since the day we met. I starved myself for you." She motioned at her body. "Lost all this weight. Got this weave. Everything to try to make you love me. Nothing I did was ever good enough. You know why? Because I'm not her!" She pointed at Rachel.

Rachel was still trying to process everything Shante said. "You hired someone to sleep with my husband?"

"Darling, it was the best money I ever spent," Shante spat.

That was the last straw. Rachel reached back with all of her might and slapped Shante as hard as she could. The blow caught Shante by surprise.

"Maybe that's why you couldn't keep your marriage together," Rachel hissed. "Because you were so busy trying to become me. You could never be me."

Shante rubbed her cheek and took a step toward Rachel. Bobby grabbed her arm. "Shante, leave her alone."

Shante stared at him before snatching her arm away. "I don't believe you. It's always about her! I can't stand neither one of you! You both will regret the day you ever hurt me!" She nearly knocked Rachel over as she stormed out.

Bobby shook his head in disbelief as he closed the door. "I'm so sorry about that, Rachel."

Rachel stood in his living room, still in shock herself.

"I had no idea she harbored that much hate," Bobby said. He stared at Rachel for a minute before easing toward her.

"Let's just try to forget about Shante, Lester, all of this drama." He reached out and put his arms around her waist. "Where were we?"

Lester had been set up? Rachel was still trying to make sense of everything. She pushed Bobby away. "I need to go."

Bobby stepped back and looked at her. "What? Why do you have to go?"

Rachel cocked her head like she had to think for a minute. "I need to go home to my husband," she said, matter-of-factly. "I need to go home. Where I belong."

"Rachel, I know you're trying to do right and all," Bobby tried to reason, "but the fact remains that he cheated on you. Set up or not, that woman didn't put a gun to his head."

Rachel was amazed that all of a sudden, Bobby didn't seem as attractive as he had just a few minutes ago. She stared at him and the only thing she could think of was her husband.

"Baby." He stepped toward her. Rachel moved out of his way.

"Bobby, seven years ago I begged you for another chance and you had your reasons for telling me no. But the fact remains that you told me no," she said as if she were coming to the realization for the first time. "And I built a life with Lester. But it's kinda like Shante said—I was never a good wife because I was pining away for you."

He grinned widely. "See, that means we were meant for one another. That's why me and Shante couldn't make it, because I was pining away for you."

"No, that just means we were both fools." Rachel could not

believe she was saying or doing what she was saying and doing. "I gotta go."

He grabbed her arm as she headed to the door. "Rachel, what about us?"

Maybe the voice that had been telling her to give up on her marriage was the devil talking, and she hadn't prayed hard enough to decipher what God really wanted her to hear. Rachel looked at Bobby's hand gripped firmly around her wrist. She used her free hand to gently remove his fingers. "Bobby, there is no us. I need you to respect that."

She looked at him one last time before she walked out the door and headed home to her husband.

chapter 46

Rachel pulled onto Interstate 10, still stunned by what Shante had told her. She had set Lester up. But did that really change anything? The bottom line was like Bobby said: Even if it was a setup, Lester still fell for it hook, line, and sinker.

Rachel's cell phone vibrated softly. Bobby had been calling her since she'd left his home but she wouldn't answer his call. She was about to press Ignore again when she noticed Twyla's number. She pressed the Talk button.

"What's going on, Twyla?"

"You tell me, Rachel," Twyla responded. "Bobby has called over here three times, something about you being over there and Shante setting up Lester. What's going on?"

Rachel sighed. "It's a long story."

"I got time," Twyla said. "First question, why were you over at Bobby's in the first place?" She waited on Rachel to reply. "Please tell me you did not sleep with him," she said when Rachel didn't say anything.

"No, I didn't sleep with him."

"Thank God."

"But I was going to."

"Rachel, how could you?" Rachel could hear the disappointment in Twyla's voice. She could no longer help it, the tears started falling.

"How could Lester do this? How could he do this to me?" Rachel cried after filling Twyla in on all the details about Shante setting Lester up. "Even if it was a setup, how could he do it?"

"But getting him back by sleeping with someone yourself isn't the answer."

"Then what is, Twyla, huh? I'm so sick of these women at the church throwing themselves at him. He's supposed to be strong. He's supposed to be like my daddy and tell these women where they can go."

"One minute you don't want him to be like your father, the next you do? The bottom line is Lester is not your father. Just like you aren't your mother."

"And then, to find out it was all a setup."

"Yeah, that's wild. I can't believe Shante would do that."

"I mean I know I did some pretty foul stuff to her, but that was years ago."

"They say you reap what you sow. Maybe it just took yours a little while to come back to you."

"Gee, thanks, Twyla."

"I'm just keeping it real with you." Twyla hesitated. "Where are you?"

"I had to stop and get some gas. But I'm on my way home now."

"Is Lester there?"

"I guess."

"Why don't you go try to put your marriage back together? I know how much you loved Bobby, but not everything we want is good for us. Lester is good for you. Whether you want to admit it or not, he's made you a better woman. You have to ask yourself what role you played in pushing him away."

"Now you sound like my daddy. It's not my fault Lester cheated."

"I'm not saying it is. But a man can only go so long without being made to feel like a man."

"What are you trying to say?"

Twyla let out a deep breath. "It's not what I'm trying to say. It's what I'm saying. You know you treat Lester like crap. He tries to treat you like a queen and you constantly beat him down. What he did wasn't right, but you know his heart."

Rachel wiped her eyes. "When did you get so wise?"

"Girl, years of dealing with James has taught me a thing or two. I know what I did to get him, I know what I have to do to keep him. Now get off this phone and go talk to your husband."

Rachel thanked her friend, then hung up. She flipped down her sun visor and surveyed herself in the mirror. She was pushing the visor back up when a loud crash sent her jerking forward.

"What in the—?"

Rachel looked up in the rearview mirror. All she could see was the bright headlights gunning toward her. The driver rammed her car again, almost causing Rachel to lose control.

Rachel's heart started racing. She firmly grabbed the steering wheel and pressed the accelerator, trying to speed away from the maniac behind her. She took one hand off the steering wheel and reached for her cell phone. She didn't know how she did it, but she managed to call 911.

"Help! Somebody is behind me trying to kill me!" she screamed in the phone.

"Where are you?" the dispatcher asked.

Rachel looked up at the sign, just as the driver hit her car again. This time, she swerved into oncoming traffic, just missing an eighteen-wheeler.

"Oh, my God!" Rachel cried.

"Ma'am, where are you?"

Rachel tried to catch her breath as she pulled the car back into her lane. "I'm on I-10, coming up on Beltway 8," she cried. "Please help me!"

"Ma'am, try to stay calm. I have an officer en route."

Tears started pouring down Rachel's face as she envisioned being run off the road, flying over an embankment or worse, having everything end in a fiery crash. She started imagining never getting a chance to say good-bye to her children, or even letting Lester know he'd been set up. Her life couldn't end like this.

Rachel looked in her rearview mirror and her tears turned to tears of joy when she saw the flashing red lights fastly approaching. The maniac must've saw it, too, because he sped up and passed Rachel.

Rachel looked over at the car. It was a black Buick with a dent in the back fender, but other than that, she couldn't make out the driver, except for the fact that it was a woman.

Rachel pulled off to the side of the freeway, shaking uncontrollably, as a police car stopped behind her. The other police car continued after the black Buick.

"Are you okay, ma'am?" the officer asked as he approached her.

Rachel continued shaking. "Somebody just tried to kill me." It suddenly dawned on her that the person who had fired at them at Johnny Carrino's wasn't aiming for her brother. They were trying to kill her. "Oh, my God."

"Ma'am, can we call someone for you?" the officer asked.

Rachel tried to shake herself out of her daze. "My husband." She handed him her cell phone. "Speed dial one. Please call my husband."

The officer called Lester. "He's on his way." He pulled out a notepad. "Now, do you have any idea who would try to run you off the road?'

Rachel took a deep breath. "I know exactly who it is. Her name is Shante Clark."

chapter 47

Rachel had never been so happy to see her husband. He must've broken every speed law under the sun because it seemed like he arrived in less than ten minutes.

They had pulled off to the service road as the officer took her statement. Lester barely gave the car time to slow down before he jumped out and came running to Rachel. "Baby! Are you okay?"

She fell into his arms, never having felt safer. "Oh, Lester, it was so terrifying."

He pulled himself from her embrace and nervously looked her up and down. "Are you sure you're okay?"

"Yeah. Just shaken up. I just want to go home. I want to hold my children."

Lester looked at the officer. "What happened?"

"Well, sir, it appears someone tried to run your wife off the road tonight." The officer snapped his notepad closed and looked at Rachel's beat-up Benz. "And from the way that Benz is battered, seems like they didn't plan on stopping until they caused some major damage."

"Why in God's name would someone want to hurt my wife?" Lester asked.

"Your wife here seems to know who it was," the officer said. "Excuse me, please. I need to go talk to someone." The officer walked away as Lester turned back to Rachel.

"Who tried to run you off the road?"

"Shante."

"Shante? As in Bobby's wife?"

"Yeah, I'm sure of it."

Lester looked confused. "Rachel, that's not possible."

Rachel shook her head. "Why not? You think she's too good to stoop to murder? You don't—"

Lester stopped her. "No, Shante couldn't be the one who tried to hurt you tonight because she was at our house when the officer called."

Rachel looked at her husband, stunned. "What? Why was she at our house?"

Lester shrugged. "She showed up there about fifteen minutes before the officer called me." Lester lowered his head. "She wanted to let me know that you were with Bobby and how much you'd hurt her. She wanted me to know," he solemnly said, "that you were most likely going to get back with Bobby, where you should've been in the first place. I had decided that she was right until the officer called and told me what happened. My heart dropped at the thought that something could've happened to you."

Rachel looked at her husband and wanted to cry. He took her hands. "Baby, I can't make you love me like you love him, but I can love you more than he can. I'm so sorry. Please give me another chance. I will spend my life making this up to you," he cried as he hugged her tightly.

Rachel pulled herself from his embrace and stared him in the eyes. Lester had loved her from the beginning. Back when she was the bad girl doing things she didn't have any business doing. Lester had been there for her when no one else had. He had loved her and her children unconditionally. And if she was honest with herself, she had to admit that she had been a less than stellar wife. She didn't know if she could make it work, but she knew she was going to try.

Rachel leaned in and kissed him. Tears began to trickle down his face revealing just how happy he was.

She began to tell him about the whole setup when it dawned on her: if it wasn't Shante who had tried to kill her, who was it?

As if on cue, a patrol car pulled up next to them. The officer parked and stepped out.

"We got a live one here," he said, motioning toward the backseat. "Caught her bailing out of the black Buick, complete with the dents in the front and white paint everywhere."

Rachel looked toward the backseat.

"It wasn't me! It was a setup! This is a conspiracy! Y'all just messing with me 'cause I'm black!"

"Tawny?"

"What, ho?" Tawny reared up and kicked the window. "What you looking at? Stank tramp. Like a freakin' cat or something with nine lives!" she yelled, and spat onto the window. "Gon' try to set me up? I got somethin' for ya! Next time, I ain't gon' miss!"

Rachel stared in disbelief.

"Come on, baby," Lester said, trying to move Rachel away.

Rachel didn't move and turned to the officer. "I thought she was in jail."

He looked at his computer screen. "It looks like she got out on a paperwork mix-up. We've been looking for her."

"Is she high?"

"As a kite," the officer replied, shaking his head. "I don't see how she was even able to drive."

"What?" Tawny kicked the window again. "Like Madea says, I ain't scared of the po-po!" Tawny started screaming at Rachel. "Watch your back. Tryin' ta set me up. I got something for ya!"

Rachel shook her head as she started to walk away. "Hey!" Tawny screamed. "Tell David to come see me on lockdown. Let him know I couldn't kill him because he my boo."

Rachel looked at Tawny, not believing this woman was for real. "Come on, Lester, let's go."

"Hey," Tawny yelled again. "Gimme a cigarette 'fo you go."

"That," Rachel said, as she and Lester walked to his car, "is your brain on drugs."

Lester smiled for the first time that evening. "Come on, baby. Let me get you home. The kids are next door at Miss Lewis's. The wrecker will take care of your car. I'm just going to run and give him the address to the body shop." He opened the passenger-side door for her and she got in.

Rachel leaned back in the seat, closed her eyes, and said a little prayer—and this time really listened as God told her she was doing the right thing by giving her husband another chance.

chapter 48

Lord, give me strength. Rachel watched Mary sashay out of the sanctuary in a skimpy little dress, trying her best to be seen.

Rachel had to take a deep breath. This woman was trying to get under her skin, plain and simple. That was all she was doing; and as Sister Morgan said, for Rachel to give in and stoop to Mary's level was simply fueling Mary's fire. Besides, after everything she'd been through the last three weeks, the last thing she needed was to let this woman get to her.

"Why is she here?" Twyla leaned in and whispered. Rachel had finally gotten Twyla to come to church more. They were standing in the church foyer mixing and mingling with other members.

"Why else? To send me over the edge." Rachel shook her head as Twyla pulled her off to the side.

"Girl, don't do it. You've been doing so good."

She *had* been doing good. She and Lester were the happiest they'd ever been. They'd been praying together, something they'd stopped doing months ago as they led their separate lives. They'd also been seeing a counselor and even though there were still many difficult days, Rachel really and truly was trying to make her marriage work. She and Lester had even taken a mini vacation to Padre Island last weekend.

"Her being here reminds me of what Lester did." Rachel sighed deeply.

"That's what she wants. You said yourself, you and Lester prayed over it and turned it over to God. Well, the devil didn't like that and he sent that Jezebel to church today."

Rachel smiled at her friend. "You sound like somebody's evangelist now."

"Girl, please. I'm just trying to tell you." She looked over at Mary, who was now standing in the line of people waiting to greet the pastor on their way out. "Do you trust Lester?"

Rachel watched Mary reach in her purse, pull out her compact, and powder her nose.

"It's hard, but I'm trying," Rachel replied.

"Don't let her set you back." Twyla frowned up at Mary, who was standing there trying to look innocent while she waited in line. "Skank."

Rachel giggled. "Excuse me, weren't you just evangelizing to me?"

Twyla rolled her eyes. "So? She's still a skank."

Rachel couldn't help it. She didn't move because she had to see how Lester would react when Mary approached him. There were two people in front of her and Mary seemed to be getting excited as a sexy smile crossed her face. Just before it was her turn, Lester motioned for the associate minister, whispered something in his ear, then quickly made an exit. The associate minister took over greeting duties for Lester and shook Mary's hand.

Rachel couldn't help but smile at the way her husband handled the situation. She was especially thrilled by the priceless look of surprise on Mary's face as she watched Lester walk off.

"Go on, Lester." Twyla laughed. "That's what I'm talking about."

Rachel was just about to respond when she looked over and saw Birdie Mae and her cohorts standing in a circle whispering as they stared back and forth between her and Mary.

She inhaled deeply. It was bad enough she had to deal with her husband's mistress; she was in no mood to deal with Birdie Mae and her crew as well, who—thanks to Layla's gossiping behind—now knew all the details about Mary and Lester's affair.

Rachel was about to make her own quick getaway when the group came stomping toward her as if they were on a mission.

"Sister Adams, may we talk to you?" Birdie Mae asked.

Normally, Rachel would've immediately gone on the defensive, but she was trying to change her attitude. So she said, "Sure."

"Well, you know everybody is talking," Birdie Mae announced. "And instead of whispering behind your back, I'm a firm believer in going straight to the source." She looked over at Mary again, who was standing around looking agitated as her eyes darted through the small crowd, no doubt looking for Lester.

"Stop beating around the bush and ask her," Norma Jean urged.

Birdie Mae shot Norma Jean a look as if to say, "I got this."

"Is it true that a certain someone"—she glanced at Mary again—"who had us praying for her, tried to mess with your husband, our beloved pastor?"

"You know, Birdie Mae, that's a personal matter that I would really rather not discuss," Rachel said, in the most sincere voice she could muster. They were probably relishing the thought that Lester had cheated on her.

"Just tell us, is that the woman you scuffled with in Lester's office?" Norma Jean blurted out.

"Yes, it is," Mary said, stepping into their conversation. "Lester and I were seeing each other. And if your *beloved* pastor thinks he can just throw me away like some piece of trash, he'd better think again."

Birdie Mae and her little group all stared Mary up and down. Rachel sighed. Why couldn't she lead a drama-free life? Rachel was just about to say something to try and squash this whole situation and get everyone out of her business, when Birdie Mae stepped toward Mary. "Look, you skinny heifer. I don't know what kind of game you're playing, but you picked the wrong first lady to mess with."

Mary's mouth dropped open, as did Rachel's.

"You might have been able to seduce my pastor once but the devil is a liar and now that we know, Pastor's got a prayer team that's gon' keep you at bay," Birdie Mae threatened.

"Amen to that," Norma Jean said as she stepped in closer.

"Don't nobody mess with our first lady," Gladys Washington added as she and Ida Hicks stepped up.

They had formed a circle around Mary and although she stood taller than all of them, the mean looks on their faces must've had her thinking twice, because her earlier confidence was gone.

"I don't believe this," Mary said. "Y'all don't even like her."

"We ain't gotta like her to love her," Birdie Mae snapped. "Bottom line is, she's family. Our church family. And you mess with a member of our family, there's gon' be hell to pay."

"And while we're all Christian women who would never dream of doing anything against God's will," Norma Jean said, balling up her pudgy little fists, "let's just say, every now and then we stray from our walk with God."

"And when we do, it ain't pretty," Gladys added.

Mary actually looked scared.

"So I would advise you to go find another church family to break up, because we here at Zion Hill don't play that," Birdie Mae growled.

Mary glanced around at all the women, before spinning around and racing out of the church.

Rachel was still in shock as Birdie Mae turned back to her.

"All of us will be watching out for her. You ain't got nothing to worry about."

Rachel didn't know what to say. "Th . . . thank you."

"Anytime, baby," Birdie Mae said. "Now you go on home and whip it on Pastor so he don't be tempted by no skinny heifers like that."

Rachel's eyes widened in shock. Birdie Mae didn't give her time to respond. She turned to her friends. "Come on, y'all. Let's go to Family Café. I sure could use some pig's feet." She walked off muttering to her friends, "That girl is crazy if she think she gon' come in here messing with our first lady."

"Done lost her mind," Ida added as they walked out of the church.

Twyla looked at Rachel. "Are those the old women you said didn't like you?"

Rachel nodded. "That's them."

"Hmph. Those are the kind of enemies I need."

Rachel couldn't help but smile. She could have never imagined in her wildest dreams what had just happened. Maybe she could get rid of the drama in her life after all.

chapter 49

"The Lord is good all the time . . ."

"And all the time the Lord is good," the congregation chanted after Lester. He had delivered a powerful sermon. Rachel had actually paid attention to most of it. She was on cloud nine as she watched her husband. Jordan and Nia had halfway behaved themselves, too. This was definitely a good day!

Simon was there, holding Brenda's hand. Rachel had to admit they looked good together. She had even hugged Brenda when they entered church.

Jonathan and Chase, David and D. J., and even Sister Morgan and the Good Girlz were here, making this day all the more special. For the first time since she could remember, Rachel actually felt at home at Zion Hill.

"Everybody say amen."

"Amen!" the congregation sang in unison.

Lester nodded toward Birdie Mae and she made her way up to the front.

"Giving honor to God, Pastor and First Lady, members and friends. It is my pleasure to stand before you today to present our first lady with a token of our appreciation for her service to Zion Hill. I know it hasn't been easy. We haven't always agreed—Lord knows I still don't understand why we need no steppers—but the young 'uns seem to like it, so I guess Sister Adams, you knew what you were doing." She smiled at Rachel.

Rachel warmly returned the gesture. She was still having a hard time believing the members were actually recognizing her in a First Lady Appreciation Ceremony. They'd sung her favorite songs. The youth had recited a poem and performed a skit. And Camille, Angel, Alexis, and Jasmine had presented her with a beautiful statue.

Deacon Baird walked up to Birdie Mae and handed her a huge bag. "On behalf of your family here at Zion Hill, we'd like to present you with this," Birdie Mae said as she held the bag out.

Rachel smiled and struggled to fight back tears as she made her way to the front. She hugged Birdie Mae, something she never in a million years ever thought she'd be doing. She then pulled the item out of the bag. It was shaped like a large picture. She pulled the wrapping paper off and her breath was taken away. It was a beautiful portrait of her, Lester, and the kids. There was a small gold plate at the bottom that read "Our First Family."

The church clapped, oooohed, and ahhhhed. Several members were teary-eyed as they stood.

"Thank you all so much," Rachel said, stepping to the microphone. "On behalf of my husband and my beautiful children, thank you."

Rachel was just about to return to her seat when Lester motioned for her to come to the podium. She leaned the picture against the wall, walked up to her husband, and stood next to him, facing the congregation. "I know it's time to go, but before we do, I needed to say a few things. As you all know, we have weathered some storms these last few months," Lester began.

"Amen," a couple of people replied.

"You ain't never lied," someone else added.

"But our God is an awesome God," Lester continued.

"That he is," Sister Hicks shouted.

Lester smiled as he took Rachel's hand. "Not only did He save my wife's life, twice, but He brought us back together and planted himself firmly at the center of our marriage."

"That's the way it should be!" someone shouted.

"That's why my wife and I feel blessed to share some joyous news with you," he continued. Rachel smiled at her husband. No, she'd never feel about him the way she'd felt about Bobby. But she'd finally realized that wasn't a bad thing.

Her love with Bobby had been an obsessive love, an unhealthy love. Her love with Lester was that agape love they talked about in First Corinthians. The kind that weathers the storms, the kind that proves that no matter what, with God at the center of your relationship, you can get through anything.

Rachel loved the glow on her husband's face. He was so excited as he prepared to share their news.

"Church, as you know we have two wonderful children." He motioned toward Jordan and Nia. "Well, now, the Lord is about to bless us with another one. Hallelujah, I'm about to be a daddy. Rachel is expecting a little one. Everybody say amen!"

Rachel smiled as she hugged her husband and "amens" chorused throughout the sanctuary. She had just pulled herself away when she looked out and saw Mary stand up and loudly proclaim, "Well, well, well. The first lady is pregnant. What do you know. Guess what? So am I. Lester, I guess you 'bout to be a daddy twice." She flashed a huge smile.

Lester's eyes grew wide. Rachel felt her knees grow weak and the last thing she remembered hearing was Sister Hicks shaking her head and saying, "Lawd have mercy, will the drama ever end?"

everybody
say
amen

ReShonda Tate Billingsley

Reading Group Guide

In this sequel to *Let the Church Say Amen,* the lovable yet troubled Jackson family is eight years older but hasn't lost its penchant for drama. Oldest son David is off drugs and trying to pull his life together, but a visit from his ex-girlfriend brings shocking news that will change his life forever. Younger brother Jonathan is locked in a heated custody battle with his ex-wife, who is still struggling to come to terms with Jonathan's sexuality. Family patriarch Simon, now retired and still shaken by his wife's passing, slowly wades into the dating pool. At the center of the novel is tempestuous daughter Rachel Jackson, who has (mostly) tamed her wild ways and settled into marriage with the newly appointed reverend of Zion Hill, Lester Adams. Although Rachel is a reluctant first lady, she plunges into her job with aplomb, debating with self-righteous church elders and forming a group for troubled teenagers. But when her first love Bobby confesses a surprising secret, Rachel's commitments to her family and her church are severely threatened.

Questions for Discussion

1. We learn at the beginning of the novel that Rachel has changed a great deal over the last few years. Her mantra is, "You are a strong, mature woman who has left those childish ways behind you. Whatever you do, do not act a fool."

How do the events of her past continue to affect her life? How do our past experiences continue to shape us, even if we try to forget them?

2. It is apparent that throughout the course of the novel Jordan has behavioral problems. Why might Jordan have been acting out? How are the children in this novel affected by the actions of their parents and other family members?

3. Did you think Angela's family's reaction to Jonathan's homosexuality was realistic? How do you think you or others you know would react in Angela's situation?

4. Simon tells Rachel, "You don't treat that man like you should . . . I know you didn't agree with your mother's philosophy that the man should be in charge of the household, but can you at least make him *feel* like he is?" Do you agree with Simon? In your experience, what is most important in making a relationship work?

5. Discuss Rachel. Did you sympathize with her? If you read the first book about the Jackson family, *Let the Church Say Amen,* do you feel differently about her after reading *Everybody Say Amen*?

6. What did you think of Bobby? Could you understand his behavior? Do you think he should have forgiven Rachel when he first learned of her affair? Do you think he wronged Shante?

7. Rachel admits that in the past she attempted to physically harm Shante and stop her marriage, and Bobby admits that he never loved Shante as much as he loved Rachel. What did you think about Shante's decision to set Lester up? Could you understand her point of view?

8. Near the end of the novel Twyla tells Rachel, "They say you reap what you sow. Maybe it just took yours a little while to come back to you." Where else does this theme appear in the novel? Do you believe this is true?

9. Did you agree with Rachel's choice to return to Lester? Do you think she was able to genuinely forgive him? If not, do you think she should have given in to her feelings for Bobby?

10. What do you think about the end of the book? Does it change your opinion of the choice Rachel made to return to Lester? Do you think Mary was telling the truth? What do you think will happen next?

11. How is forgiveness an important theme in this novel? Consider the relationships between Tawny and David, Angela and Jonathan, and Rachel and Bobby.

12. Could you relate to any character more than the others? Did you feel that any character was the novel's moral center?

Questions for the Author

From the suspenseful way this novel ends, it seems that we might not have heard the last of the Jackson family. Are you working on another sequel?

I know this may sound crazy, but the characters in my books talk to me and tell me when they're ready to continue their story. So far, Rachel hasn't told me she's ready to let the world know what happened from here. But if I know Rachel, I'm sure she will.

How did you come up with these characters? Are they based on people you know? Rachel is a very realistic and multi-faceted character. How did you approach writing her?

Everyone wants to know who Rachel is. She's your best friend, sister, cousin, the girl down the street or even (gasp) you. (Although most people will never admit it. But tell the truth, you or someone you know has thought about pulling one of her dirty tricks before.) Rachel was a combination of people I know and my very active imagination. I wrote about her as if I were a friend simply telling her story.

What was it like to revisit these characters in a new book? Had you always intended to write a sequel to *Let the Church Say Amen*?

No, I didn't intend on writing a sequel. But again Rachel told me she had matured and she wanted people to see the new side, to show a woman can actually turn around her crazy childish ways. The readers also demanded a sequel. They wanted to know more and as a writer, I felt a responsibility to give that to them.

Do you sympathize most with any of your characters?

I actually feel for Rachel because she was a young girl looking for love in all the wrong places, and when she found it she didn't know how to appreciate it. I also sympathize with Jonathan because I can only imagine what it's like to carry the burden he did.

You have written a successful inspirational series for teenagers. Do you prefer writing for teenagers or adults?

I enjoy both, actually. Writing for teenagers allows me to intro-duce young people to reading and helps them to develop a love for reading. By only complaint about writing for teenagers is that I've found I'm not as hip as I thought as I was. (Hey, in my world, people still say 'da bomb.') I love my adult stories because that's what I read and my adult fans are the ones who made my career what it is.

There is a lot of empathy in this book, even between characters who don't understand each other at all. Do you feel that you're a particularly empathetic and forgiving person in your own life? Which authors have most inspired you in your life and your writing?

I'm very empathetic. My family says sometimes too much so. And I definitely think it's reflected in my life and my writing. Because I read a lot, there are so many authors who have inspired me, but the one who spurred my desire to share my stories was Maya Angelou.

What are you currently reading?

My next Good Girlz book!

What role does the church play in your life? Has it always been an important element of your life?

Actually, I was raised in the church and my foundation is built on faith. So that is reflected in my writing.

How did you used to balance your journalism career, writing career, and your family? Was your goal always to write fiction full-time? Do you ever miss being in the newsroom?

I'm a firm believer in utilizing every spare moment, from dictating on a tape recorder at a stoplight or writing notes at the doctor's office. I manage to do it all by not sitting around idly. I believe every moment you spend talking about how you don't have time to do something could be used doing something. I never actually expected to become a full-time writer because I enjoyed the newsroom so much but God had other plans. Now, while I miss the news business a bit, I feel like I've realized my true life calling as a writer.

You were extremely successful in self-publishing your early books. Would you recommend self-publishing for up-and-coming authors?

Absolutely, I truly believe you should let no one but you and God determine your destiny. If you're sitting waiting for a publisher or agent to validate your talents, your story may never be told, you could be waiting forever. Self-publishing allows you the opportunity to share your work with the world. But I have to encourage those who are considering it, give it your all. Put out a professional product. Treat it as a mainstream piece of work and everything else will fall into place.

Enhance Your Book Club

1. Have a potluck dinner and bring your favorite home-cooked Sunday dinner dishes. Find any recipe you need at http://www.foodnetwork.com, from savory main courses to delectable desserts.

2. In the spirit of Rachel's work with teenage girls, organize a volunteer day. Check out http://www.volunteermatch.org or http://www.volunteersolutions.org for ideas.

3. Learn more about the author at http://www.reshonda tatebillingsley.com and www.myspace.com/reshonda_tate_ billingsley. Look for upcoming tour dates!